TALES FROM THE

Haunted Mansion

TALES FROM THE
Haunted Mansion

Volume IV
Memento Mori

Transcribed by *John Esposito*
as told by mansion librarian *Amicus Arcane*
Illustrations by *Kelley Jones*

DISNEP PRESS
Los Angeles • New York

ISBN 978-1-368-06526-9
FAC-025393-20197

Printed in Guangdong, China
First Hardcover Edition, July 2019
First Box Set Edition, July 2020
1 3 5 7 9 10 8 6 4 2

For more Disney Press fun, visit www.disneybooks.com

Introduction

50th ANNIVERSARY

The Haunted Mansion

Welcome, foolish mortals, to
our grand anniversary celebration.

The party began on August 9, 1969,
when 999 happy haunts
from crypts throughout the world
retired to the spooky sanctum of our humble abode,
the Haunted Mansion.

The frightening festivities have continued ever since,
both above ground and below,
in this country and beyond.

For the foolish mortals brave enough to attend,
we guarantee a ghoulishly good time.
And the haunting's free,
so please join our jamboree.

Your doom buggy awaits. . . .

Welcome

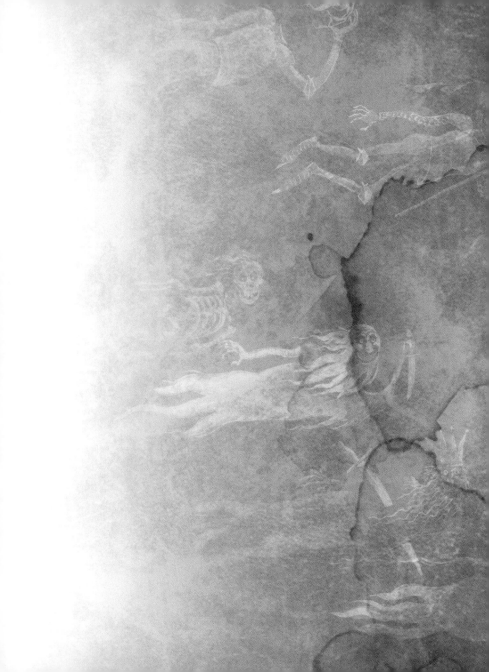

THE END IS NIGH.

All things must pass, foolish reader. It is
the law of the universe . . . and of regions
beyond. Every beginning has an end.

As each day turns to night and every body turns to dust, so, too, must my tenure as your loyal librarian reach its creepy conclusion.

All things must pass.

Yes, I, Amicus Arcane, keeper of frightening fictions and your ghost host for these tales, shall be moving on to grayer pastures. It has been my distinct displeasure to serve you—the living—to regale your kind with 999 spooky stories from creepy crypts around the globe.

But before I go, I have one final service to attend. It is my obligation as departing librarian to select a replacement, someone—or something—to keep watch over our diabolical depository.

How about you, foolish reader? Do you have what it takes? Will you be our next librarian? I am seeking just the right nightmarish note on which to end. So bring me your scariest tale.

But be warned—the competition is stiff. Quite literally. Ghost writers from around the world will be vying for the position. Final arrangements have been made, invitations have been sent, doom buggies have been dispensed. At the stroke of thirteen, the first guests shall appear—and disappear.

Won't you join us?

You are cordially invited to attend this grand celebration.

The entrance should be frighteningly familiar by now.

You enter by turning the page.

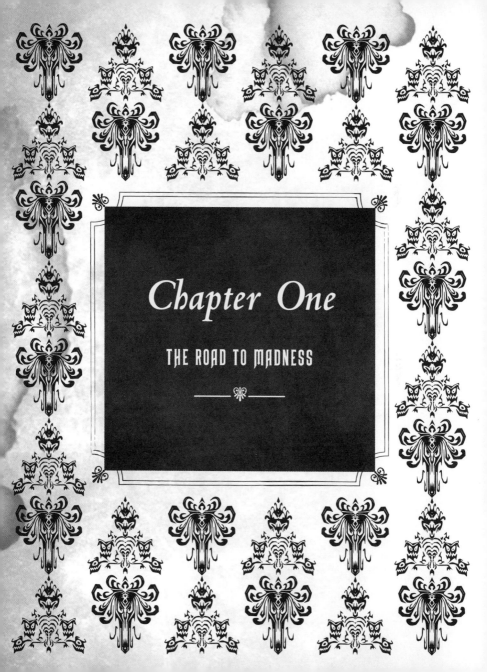

Chapter One

THE ROAD TO MADNESS

Who would pave such a path? What pestilent purpose could it serve? It is said that all roads lead somewhere. Route 13, with its curving, twisting, winding lane perpetually blanketed by a debilitating fog, can only lead to madness.

Or death.

It has led to madness and death before, many times during its storied past. *And it soon will again.*

Thirteen people died during its inception. That's how the treacherous path, whose actual name is no longer spoken, got its unofficial moniker. Countless motorists have gone missing trying to navigate its corrupt course, as tributes littering both sides of the road attest. There have been numerous sightings, now considered folklore, of specific apparitions. The most common one involves a trio of mischievous hitchhikers looking to bum a ride from unsuspecting travelers. Local legends, of course. Legends that have no basis in fact. Or do they?

Apart from those transcendental sightings, the dense foliage that hugs Route 13 is home to peculiar wildlife—bats, ravens, and vultures, to name but a few—nocturnal in nature. Like the road itself, its surroundings thrive in darkness.

Legend has it that beyond the vestige of a vast cemetery, the path leads to a gated mansion on a hill. For those who make it past its threshold, a wondrous journey awaits. The mansion is said to be the doorway to a world yet to come, a place beyond one's darkest imaginings. Souls from around the globe, it's been whispered, go there to "retire"—some by choice, others by more persuasive methods. For those willing to embrace its magic, there are myriad rewards: a return to the wonders of childhood, a confirmation of those dark imaginings.

But to the nonbelievers—beware! To those who doubt:

turn back now. If you dismiss the indisputable evidence of a world beyond ours, a much graver fate awaits.

A fate worse than death.

Officer Davis was new to the police department. It was only his second night on the job when the terror began. The new ones were always given the night shift. And the brand-new ones were always given Route 13 to see if they had what it took to make it on the force. Davis had heard all the rumors, of course, the ones about Route 13 being—what was the word?—*frilly*. No, that wasn't the word.

Treacherous. The word was *treacherous*.

A word that suited Officer Davis just fine. Because along with *treacherous* came *deserted*. Very few travelers ventured onto Route 13 after dark. The daytime was a different matter. Route 13 was the only road going into and out of the Eternal Grace Cemetery.

Officer Davis didn't punch in till midnight. We're talking the late, late shift. The witching hour, as they call it. He had parked his squad car behind a USE CAUTION AFTER DARK billboard, keeping strategically out of sight. His job was to protect the roadway. But there were no speeders that night apart from several large bats fluttering past his radar, and he couldn't ticket them.

It was going to be a very dull shift, with plenty of time to catch up on his reading. Officer Davis was dying to know how his book ended. It was one of those horror anthologies most respectable readers wouldn't be caught dead with. **Aaaah! You've been caught. Play dead!** It involved a group of friends who loved to tell scary stories. It was called *The Gruesome Group*. **Not The Fearsome Foursome. Copyright issues, you understand.**

Officer Davis opened the book and skimmed all the way to the end. It was the fourth and final tale, and it involved a premature burial. Davis smiled appreciatively. *Those horror writers. Where did they get their sick ideas?* He flipped over the book and studied the author photo: a rosy-cheeked lady with thick glasses, her silver hair worn in a bun. Truthfully, she looked about as menacing as your local librarian. **Ahem!** Hers wasn't a face you'd associate with such tales, and in fact, her bio stated she had once been a poetess. Of course, penning tales about the unliving was way more profitable, so she switched gears. And it was a good thing, too. Her stories had already been translated into 666 languages; even an awful movie adaptation couldn't tarnish her brand. We're talking, of course, about that international icon of fright: Prudence Pock, who,

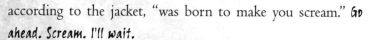

according to the jacket, "was born to make you scream." **Go ahead. Scream. I'll wait.**

AAAAAAAAAAAHHHHH!

Was that you?

The book flew out of Officer Davis's hands. The scream, a genuine cry of terror, had come from somewhere along Route 13. His heart was racing—so fast, in fact, he could have given it a speeding ticket.

AAAAAAAAAAAAAAAHHHHH!

There it was again, longer and louder. Someone needed help. So Officer Davis grabbed his flashlight and hopped out of the car.

The road felt unnatural, as if he was heading downward instead of upward. Officer Davis was afraid; he'd be the first to admit that. **Would you be the second?**

Cruuuuunch. Crunch. Cruuunch. Cruuuunch.

Uh-oh. He heard footsteps, the crunchy kind, headed his way. "Is somebody there?" His flashlight hand was trembling. "Hello?" He made a half-turn, maneuvering his light. "Show yourself, whoever you are. If you're in trouble, I can help!" It was his first real police officer moment. And also his last. He would resign the next day, like everyone else who'd worked the night shift on Route 13. But at least he *sounded* in charge.

He wasn't, of course. *Cruuunch. Crrrrrrrunch.* The footsteps were in charge. The night belonged to them.

Caw! Caw! Caw! Another sound emerged from the trees. Davis looked up and saw a large raven eyeballing him from a branch. *Caw! Caw! Caw!*

He agreed with the bird. It was time to get back to the car—car—car! He bolted down the hill, which felt like he was bolting up the hill. *Could things get any worse?* he thought. Then his flashlight went out.

They could.

The squad car was just ahead, shrouded in fog. He made it to the door and leaped inside. Safe! Officer Davis slumped down below the steering wheel, closing his eyes for a second of relief. With his eyes closed, he couldn't see the skeletal hand creeping up over the seat behind him. But soon he felt its bony digits making a path across his shoulder.

"Good evening, Officer," someone said from the backseat.

Officer Davis jerked forward, and his breath left his body. Looking up into his rearview mirror, he saw a skull-like face glaring back at him—grinning. He flipped on the interior lights and turned, finding a fully fleshed woman in place of the skeleton. "Who are you?" he demanded.

"Don't you know?"

Looking over his shoulder, he saw a face he recognized. In fact, he'd just been admiring her picture. Prudence Pock, author of *The Gruesome Group*, was inside the car. "They're coming for me, Officer. The spirits of the dead. And then they'll come for *you*." Prudence Pock added a laugh, the scary kind nobody likes to hear.

Officer Davis hit the gas, and as the squad car raced from Route 13, he radioed headquarters and informed them of the situation. Upon hearing the crazed laughter over the radio, headquarters advised him to take Prudence Pock directly to Shepperton Sanitarium, an asylum for the insane.

The staff at Shepperton referred to the ward below the basement as the dungeon. It was where they kept the special patients, the ones the doctors deemed incurable. The laughers and the screamers. The ones they would never allow to leave.

It was several hours past mealtime—an unusual time to be in an unusual place. The overhead fluorescents brought an unnatural brightness to the sparse corridor. An elevator door opened at the far end, and a pair of properly dressed gentlemen entered the chilled domain. The first was Coats, the night orderly. He punched a security code into a keypad with his gloved hand. There was a buzz followed by a mechanized release. A set of security doors swished open, and the orderly extended his hand. "This way, Dr. Ackerman."

The esteemed Dr. Ackerman was behind him. An acclaimed psychiatrist and author, Dr. Ackerman was considered the leading expert on the incurably insane. The doctor waited, somewhat impatiently, as the orderly lit the individual candles of an antique candelabrum. "Really, Coats. That's a bit theatrical, don't you think?"

"Theatrical, sir?"

"The candles. It's perfectly light down here."

"For now." The orderly led Dr. Ackerman into the narrow passage. "The lights get temperamental during storms. Take my word for it, Doctor. You don't want to be down here in the dark."

The doctor sighed. "Very well. Lead on."

The hall was sixty feet long, made of cinder blocks, with six numbered doors, three on either side. They were entrances to padded rooms, each one equipped with a small rectangular observation slot. The sole accoutrement was a round clock on the far wall, its face protected by steel mesh. Ackerman thought that beyond its modern facade, the same corridor might have been an actual dungeon back in the day, its padded cells torture chambers equipped with devices such as the rack and the knee splitter. *Ah! Did someone say "party games"?*

A patient barked out orders as Dr. Ackerman passed his door. "Martin! I'll take my tea now, Martin! Original blend! Chop-chop!"

"It's not quite teatime, Colonel," replied the orderly. Dr. Ackerman looked his way, curious. "That would be Colonel Tusk," explained the orderly. "The famous importer of rare and exotic goods. He's been with us for quite some time."

"Why, may I ask? He sounds perfectly lucid."

The orderly moved close, the flickering candelabrum bringing an unnatural glow to his gaunt face. "Some time back, he imported an Egyptian mummy to the States. Along with some very special tea leaves. And, well, the details are in his file." *As well as Volume III.*

"Making progress, I trust?"

The orderly lowered his head. "I'm afraid he's lost, sir. Like the others. Trapped in the recesses of his own mind. You see, the residents of the dungeon"—his eyes shifted to the other doors—"they share an uncommon trait."

"And that trait would be?"

"They say they've seen a ghost, good doctor. Or two.

Or three." A thunderclap rocked the hallway, a bone-rattling rumble, taking out the overhead lights. The orderly lifted the candelabrum, his face saying *I told you so*, followed by his mouth: "I told you so." The orderly pointed to a door labeled 4. "She's in there, sir. Our newest arrival. Been requesting you by name."

"That's odd. Do I know the patient?"

"Perhaps by her work. You are a reader, are you not?"

"Yes. As a matter of fact, it's a favorite pastime."

"Ah! It's good to pass the time, Doctor. Since time is all we have . . . in the end." The orderly inserted a brass skeleton key into the lock. But before he turned the latch, the door creaked open on its own.

The encompassing walls of room 4 were made up of small white cubes, making it look like the inside of a giant igloo, with no windows and no d—Well, there was one door, if we're being honest. The orderly carried a stool in from the corridor and set it down. "Dr. Ackerman to see you, Mistress Pru—" He stopped himself. "Ma'am."

The patient was seated on her own stool with her back to them. Dr. Ackerman could see her silvery bun bobbing up and down. She was busy doing something. "I'll just be a minute. It's almost finished." Prudence Pock looked as though she was writing, but she had no pen and no paper. She was writing a story on air.

Dr. Ackerman sized her up. If appearances counted for anything, she looked to be mild-mannered, a middle-aged woman. The doctor turned to the orderly, who remained in the doorway. "You can leave now, Coats. I'm certain patient four will behave."

"Very well," replied the orderly. "I'll be right outside if you need me. All you have to do is scream." Dr. Ackerman heard the key turn the latch. He was locked in a padded room with patient four.

Dr. Ackerman placed his stool directly across from Prudence, smiling when he caught her eye. "What are you working on?"

"A tale."

"I'd be interested in hearing it. Would you care to tell me what it's about?"

"When it's finished." Her hand kept moving, and Dr. Ackerman kept waiting. He waited until she appeared to complete her invisible work. "Ahhh, that one creeped me out!" she said, and mimed putting down a pen.

Dr. Ackerman tried changing the subject. Something

mundane. Sane. "I'm told you haven't taken a meal. Perhaps now that you've completed your work . . ."

"I seem to have permanently lost my appetite. Why do you suppose that is, Doctor? What is your prognosis?"

She was baiting the doctor, but he refused to bite. "Let's chat a bit first. May I sit?"

"Be my guest."

Dr. Ackerman lowered himself onto the stool. "I understand you requested to see me."

They locked eyes, and Dr. Ackerman had a momentary flash of recognition. He knew her face; it had once been a very famous one. This pleased Prudence Pock. "There, Doctor. You do know me."

"From your books. And, of course, I've seen you on some talk shows. Mostly around Halloween."

"Yes, that is my busy season." She slid her stool closer. "Do you consider yourself a fan?"

The question caught the doctor off guard, and it gave her enormous pleasure to see him squirm. "This isn't about me, my dear. It's about you."

"But I'm familiar with your work, too, Doctor. I know everything you've done."

Dr. Ackerman nodded appreciatively. He was an author

in his own right, with thirteen nonfiction best sellers under his belt, each one focused on a specific incurable madness. It made sense for a purveyor of terror tales to use his books as research.

"Tell me, Doctor. You're highly educated. Do you believe in an afterlife?"

Dr. Ackerman took a long breath. He could feel the orderly watching through the door slot. He needed to be careful. He knew from experience the wrong response usually set the quiet ones off. He gave his stock answer. "What I believe is unimportant. It's what you believe, my dear. That's the only truth I'm interested in."

"Aaah, the truth. That is important." Prudence Pock removed her glasses. There was an unmistakable certainty in her eyes, her look never wavering. "Memento mori."

"Beg your pardon?"

"Me-men-to mor-i," she repeated, savoring every syllable. "Are you familiar with the term?"

The doctor had a general idea. "It's Latin, of course. If memory serves, it means 'Remember death.'" He added under his breath, "As if one could forget it."

"You're close, Doctor. So very close. It means 'Remember you must die.'"

He resented the correction, as minor as it was. "And these words—they hold some special significance?"

"All words pertaining to death hold significance for me. Death is my business, Doctor. At least, it *was*. Graves, ghouls, goblins—they were my bread and butter."

"But you stopped. Why?"

She looked at him sharply, then smiled, as if he'd made an unexpected blunder. "Come now, Doctor. You're my biggest fan. You know a lot more than you're admitting to. That's fine. I'll play your little game. In truth, I hadn't produced a worthwhile sentence in years."

"Why do you suppose that is?"

"I suppose . . . I stopped believing." She rose to her feet, making the six-foot-two Dr. Ackerman feel small. "I stopped believing in the ghosts and the goblins that populated my work. And when a writer stops believing, the words stop believing. The inkwell goes dry, so to speak."

"You're talking about writer's block." Dr. Ackerman stood, too.

"Yes, Doctor. Writer's block. I no longer believed in anything I had to say. Until that night in the mansion. The things I saw, Doctor. The visions of a world I dare not convey. If my readers only knew . . . they'd never sleep again."

"Why is that? Why would your readers never sleep again?"

She shifted her eyes to the rectangular slot in the door. "Because, dear doctor . . . they'd be too busy praying."

Prudence Pock had gotten under his skin, all right.

"What's wrong, Doctor? You seem distressed."

He avoided looking at her eyes—eyes that told the truth. They were the windows to Prudence's soul and perhaps to his, too.

"Please sit down, Doctor. You're making me anxious."

"Very well, if it will calm your nerves." Dr. Ackerman returned to his stool, and in the same moment, both of them sat. "Do you know why they brought you here?" he asked.

"Of course, Doctor. They say I'm *unsane*."

Dr. Ackerman paused, almost as if for dramatic effect. "I'll be the judge of that. Let's start from the beginning, shall we?"

"Where to begin?" Prudence smiled wistfully, thinking back forty-eight hours. "I suppose it all began in Liberty Square. I was doing an event in a small brick-and-mortar shop. A book signing."

"Something new?"

His question amused her. "Now, now, Doctor. I already told you, I haven't written anything new in years. It's a compilation of short stories. Some of my early work. A greatest hits package, if you will. *The Very Best of Prudence Pock.* Sound familiar?"

"No," he lied, "I'm afraid I don't know that one."

There was a moment of silence. Then Prudence slapped her hands together. *CLAP!* The doctor jolted back, startled. "So sorry, Doctor. I didn't mean to frighten you . . . prematurely." She opened her hands, and the color drained from the doctor's face. There was an old hardcover book in her hands; it seemed to have appeared out of nowhere.

"That's remarkable. How did you do that?"

"Magic, Dr. Ackerman. I believe in magic again. And before this night is out, so will you. Now, where were we?"

Prudence Pock leaned forward and started from the beginning. From the event in Liberty Square two days earlier.

The last time she had been considered sane.

Chapter Two

YOU ARE CORDIALLY INVITED

It was in Ye Olde Book Shoppe that Prudence Pock first came to a numbing realization: *It's almost over.* The first visible signs of arthritis had crept in. Her joints were gnarled, her fingers twisted. It was becoming painful just to sign her name. *Soon I'll have to give up the pen,* she thought. *The quill. The instrument of my art. And how many people will actually care?*

How many people would actually care? Thirty-one fans had shown up in total. You wouldn't call it a crowd, but hey, has-beens can't be choosers. And wasn't it better to be a has-been than a never-was? Her reading public had moved on to a new flavor. And who could blame them? Not Prudence Pock.

She was grateful for the handful of fans she had left.

The next person in line held out a book for her to sign. He was a high school freshman, at most. Couldn't even make eye contact. "Who would you like it made out to?" she asked.

His response was barely audible. "Just your name, please." Prudence signed her name and slid the book across the table. She knew the autograph wasn't for him. He planned to sell it online. Turn a fast buck. The young ones weren't interested.

Ouch!

Prudence Pock knew the sting of rejection all too well. It had been her partner, her mate, for most of her professional life. A lifetime of strangers telling her that her work wasn't good enough. That they liked the last one better. That what she said or did had no value. But for that one crumb, that tiny morsel, had any of it truly been worth it?

"I'm your biggest fan." Prudence heard it as an angelic whisper. And in that instant, she decided it had. It had been worth it. She looked up, adjusting her glasses to greet the fan.

But there was no one there, just the soft tinkling of a charm bracelet still lingering in the air. It reminded Prudence of her childhood. In place of a book, there was a small black envelope with a fancy seal: AA stamped in bloodred wax.

—

Prudence stepped outside Ye Olde Book Shoppe, holding her complimentary mochaccino, hoping to see the mystery girl riding off on a pretty pink bike with a wicker basket stuffed with fancy invites. But Liberty Square had pretty much cleared out. She glanced back at the shop. The manager was already plucking down the banner that announced her signing: PRUDENCE POCK——MISTRESS OF THE MACABRE! BORN TO MAKE YOU SCREAM!

The fancy black envelope was no bigger than an index card, probably an invitation to a kid's birthday party. Prudence loosened the seal with her stirrer and removed a card. It was an invitation, most certainly, but not to a child's party. In deep red lettering, it read:

Dear Mistress Prudence:
You are cordially invited to attend a ghost writers' symposium.
A grand prize will be bestowed upon the author of the scariest tale,
to be selected by yours truly.
A carriage will be sent to collect you tomorrow evening
when the Liberty Square clock tower strikes twelve.
We're dying for you to attend.
Sincerely,
Amicus Arcane,
H.M. librarian

Prudence shuddered when she saw the name (*thank you*), then looked across the village square to see if she was being pranked. No signs of that. She slipped the invitation back inside the envelope, considering its implications. What if it wasn't a prank? And the grand prize. What could it be? Then she thought about what her life had become.

Most evenings were spent in front of a TV, watching old Diana Durwin movies and eating microwave dinners. She couldn't remember the last time she'd been invited out. Why shouldn't she attend? To go out and socialize? It might be fun. Certainly different. Maybe even adventurous. These days, what did she have to lose? *I could say, but why spoil the ending?*

And that was when Prudence Pock accepted the invitation to a grand celebration that would change her life—maybe even shorten it—forever and ever.

Twenty-four hours later, Prudence found herself back in Liberty Square, watching the minute hand on the clockface creep toward midnight. She was waiting for her ride to what she guessed would be a strange and wondrous evening. She had chosen a simple black dress—one she hadn't worn since the death of her beau—with a light sweater in case she got the chills. Somehow, it felt appropriate.

Gong!

The clock struck twelve and the air itself seemed to part, allowing for the introduction of a different sound. It was the clip-clop of hooves, and Prudence Pock couldn't believe what she was seeing.

An old-fashioned carriage had approached the square and was making its way over to its *soul* passenger. It creaked to a halt directly in front of her, a motorless antique hearse, out of fashion since the nineteenth century. All black, naturally, with an oblong compartment made of see-through glass.

Prudence smiled appreciatively. She had to hand it to this Amicus Arcane, whoever he was. He'd certainly gotten the fine details right. There was even a dead wreath attached to the rear, with a flowing sash that read WITH OUR DEEPEST CONDOLENCES. She stepped around front to greet the driver. But there wasn't one. Doubly strange, there wasn't even a horse. Just a harness floating in midair where a horse should be. But she'd heard the clopping, right? *Right?*

She added light applause to her smile. "Bravo! Bravo!" Clearly, someone had been operating the hearse by remote control from somewhere nearby. That would be one explanation. But not the only one.

Prudence reached for the door handle, and not surprisingly,

the door opened on its own. She squeezed herself into the oblong compartment and had to lie down horizontally to fit. After all, it was meant for a coffin. As soon as she settled in, the hearse jerked forward, the clopping of invisible hooves echoing through Liberty Square.

And almost instantly, Prudence felt her writer's block disappear. The creative juices were flowing again, flowing like rivers of blood.

The horseless hearse coasted through town, passing a quaint gazebo, where local teens had their first kisses, and Rosie's Ice Cream Shop, where local kids had their first scoops. Villagers were lining the sidewalk, even at so late an hour, eyeing the hearse like the main float in a paranormal parade. Some of the gentlemen even removed their hats. Perhaps they thought it was a real funeral. *So this is how the dead feel,* thought Prudence. *Respected.* She liked that.

But it was the marquee on the recently restored Bijou theater that sent torrents of ice water through her veins, its melty red letters dripping, bleeding, pleading:

NOW PLAYING:

MEMENTO MORI

The journey continued up that treacherous path most often referred to as Route 13, where ravens cawed and blackened trees reached out to grab travelers. It was the kind of road Prudence used to write about, before the affliction took hold—a path perpetually mired in fog, its only source of light an almost impossibly large moon shimmering through dead branches. She had visited Route 13 many times in the past. What respectable ghost writer hadn't? Her first time was when she was doing research for a story on those legendary hitchhiking ghosts, one of whom was a distant relation. *But that's a whole other story.*

Prudence found herself heading for the wrought iron gates of the Eternal Grace Cemetery, one of the oldest, most distinguished boneyards in the land. But the gates were chained shut and the horseless hearse was moving fast, way too fast to stop. Prudence Pock could see it coming. The horrible accident! The tiny obituary! It was a foregone conclusion, the collision inevitable. Add the death of Prudence Pock to the lurid legacy of Route 13.

She closed her eyes. No time for prayers.

But she never felt an impact, because the impact never came. Prudence opened her eyes and looked out through the glass enclosure. There were gravestones whizzing by her. Somehow, some way, the horseless hearse had passed through the gate without crashing.

The hearse arrived at her final destination, and Prudence departed prematurely—in the most literal sense—and watched as the horseless hearse clip-clopped off, disappearing into the fog. Looking around brought about a shiver. The fog, the moon, the sounds. It felt like a moment from one of her stories. She could see the headlines: *Famous ghost writer stranded in graveyard.* Stranded, yes. But not alone.

She heard festive music emerging from beyond the tombstones. For a city of the dead, the graveyard was especially hopping!

Bagpipes, harps, flutes, and tambourines. Prudence rubbed her hands together. It was that curious combination of fear and excitement. She didn't know what she expected to see. Something good? Something bad? But the time for guessing had passed. She made her way along a footpath, examining the headstones—most with amusing epitaphs—as she went.

A large one featured the sculpted semblance of a woman, her hair carefully intertwined with a shroud that wrapped around her disembodied noggin. Prudence felt a pang when she read whose ghostly retreat it was.

DEAR SWEET LEOTA,
BELOVED BY ALL
IN REGIONS BEYOND NOW,
BUT HAVING A BALL

It was the final resting place of the world's most powerful medium. And Prudence thought, *Rand would have just died to see this!* **He did.** At the same time, the sculpted likeness winked! Prudence chuckled nervously. A common defense mechanism. Chuckles instead of screams. **Not to worry, foolish reader. The screams are on their way.**

For now, the festivities were underway. She could see colored balls of light—orbs to those in the know—bouncing jubilantly in the night sky! Were her eyes playing tricks on her? The images were beyond her darkest imaginings, and just a reminder: she could imagine *very dark*. Frightful figures were everywhere. One resembled a living mummy sitting up in a sarcophagus and sipping a cup of tea. And over yonder! A king and a queen were balancing on a seesaw. And what of the five marble busts, singing their merry song—some ditty about *grim grimy hosts coming out to soak their eyes*. **Ahem! Let's get that hearing checked, shall we, Mistress Prudence?**

Marvelous, thought Prudence. *The special effects are simply marvelous.* Because what other explanation could there be? Sights such as those weren't real. The frightful figures had to be holograms, or some sort of state-of-the-art animatronics. Special effects to die for! **Quite literally.**

Clink-tink-clink.

Prudence heard the sound, one she recognized from the bookshop. The clinking of jewelry, most likely a charm brace-let. She turned to spot the owner. Instead, Prudence found herself looking into the eyes of a granite angel perched on a pedestal, its wings expanded, its hair seeming to change colors in the moonlight.

The girl depicted by the statue looked so young, so lovely, so innocent. **A guess, a guess, and a guess.**

Prudence stepped closer to read the marker, and her eyes filled with tears. "Twelve years old. My poor, sweet angel. You had your whole life ahead of you." She took a step back and saw the bracelet. But it wasn't possible. It had been sculpted around the statue's wrist, the charms representing various pets: a rabbit, a parrot, a goldfish, and a guinea pig. "They showed you love, didn't they? At least you had love." And she might have added *unlike me.*

Prudence stroked the angel's cheek. But the melancholy moment was rudely interrupted when something flicked her silvery bun. Prudence turned to scold whoever it was. She saw no one, but she heard laughter. The impish chortles of mischievous boys. Where were they hiding?

As Prudence turned back to regard the angel one last time, her jaw nearly hit the ground. **Pick up on aisle thirteen!** The stone angel had disappeared, utterly and completely, as if it had flown off. Only the pedestal remained.

Clink-tink-clink.

The sound approached from above. Prudence smiled, forgetting where she was. She'd always wanted to meet an angel. But then the smile went away. *Aren't angels merely devils in disguise?* she wondered.

She located a small reserve of courage and turned to face whatever it might be. She didn't see a devil. Not yet, anyway. She saw a young girl, no more than twelve, with blue hair and eyes that matched. The embodiment of the granite angel, minus the wings. "Hello, there," said the girl in a voice Prudence remembered from her signing.

"Hello." It was especially chilly, so Prudence removed her sweater and offered it to the blue-haired stranger. "Take it, sweetie. You'll catch your death out here."

The girl couldn't help giggling. "I seriously doubt that."

Prudence nodded, slipping her arms back into the cardigan. "Those boys I heard—are they with you?"

"The little jerkoids! Did they scare you?"

"No, not really." Prudence smiled. "Just boys being boys."

The girl shook her head like a disapproving den mother. "Those boys, as you call them, are a lot older than they appear. I sometimes wish—" She cut herself off with a painful reminder: *No more wishes.*

"Are you here visiting a loved one?"

The girl shook her head. "I'm here visiting you." Prudence noticed the silver bracelet around her wrist, glistening in the moonlight. *Clink-tink-clink.*

"You're the one. The girl who left me the invitation."

"That's me," the angelic presence confirmed. And she added, "I'm your biggest fan. I've read all your work, even the things you haven't written yet. Tonight, if you'll allow me . . . I'd like to inspire you."

Prudence was both curious and confused, trying to make sense of it all and figure out where it was going. *Stop guessing. See Volumes I, II, and III.*

"I don't understand," she finally responded. "What are you trying to say?"

"It's much better if I show you." The girl pointed to the horizon. *Clink-tink-clink.* "It isn't very far."

"What isn't very far?"

"The place you've always dreamed of."

A pathway appeared between the headstones, zigzagging all the way up the hill. The blue-haired girl led the way, Prudence seeing her angelic form floating behind stone monuments.

"Wait!" Prudence ran to catch up. "Slow down! These knees aren't what they used to be!" The girl paused, hovering as if she was standing on air. "I just realized," Prudence said between huffs and puffs, "I don't even know your name."

The girl smiled. It had been so long since anyone had asked. "Willa," she replied. And in that moment, her hair returned to its natural color, dirty blond.

Willa. Willa Gaines. That was the name Prudence had seen on the marker. And the very idea of it greatly disturbed her. "Look, dear. I enjoy a good scare just as much as the next girl, but using the name of a dead person seems in pretty poor taste."

"It's my real name, *dear*. And while we're on the subject of poor taste, let's discuss those books you wrote. *The Gruesome Group.*"

"What about them?"

"They were based on real kids, too, weren't they?"

Prudence was flustered, as if she'd just been caught with her hand in the cookie jar. **Or is it "cookie in the hand jar"? I never can get that right.** "That's completely unfair."

"Oh, yeah? Why is that, Prudence Pock?"

"Well, for starters, I changed all the names. Along with most of the details."

"Oh, you want details?" And for a flash, the angelic young girl took on the spectral image of a corpse, gnawed on by various animals. *Clink-tink-clink.* Prudence turned away, not wanting to believe. And in an instant, the angelic Willa had returned. "The real kids called themselves the Fearsome Foursome," she explained. "Would you like to know where *they* ended up?"

Prudence lowered her head out of respect. "I, uh, think we all know where they ended up." She heard those boys again, their impish laughter moving among headstones.

Willa pointed to a patch of blank sky. "They ended up there."

Prudence saw nothing, nothing but sky. "I don't see anyth—"

"Try harder," insisted Willa. "It's a place you've written about. A place you've seen in your dreams."

Caw! Caw! Caw!

Prudence spun around. A large black raven had been watching them from the top of an old crypt, the surname ARCANE arched above the entrance. She regained her composure and, once again, looked to the sky where Willa was pointing.

This time, she saw a solitary structure—a mansion—perched high on a hill. It hadn't been there a second before; of that she was certain. "By God, it's real! The place Rand was searching for!" And by God, it was! Real, that is. The mansion had been waiting for her, waiting all those years for Prudence to find her way. She could feel the lure of its enigmatic embrace. It was inviting her into its unhallowed halls, tempting her to partake in its devious delights. **Welcome, dear Prudence. Enter freely and of your own will. . . .**

"Am I imagining this? Or is it all a dream within a dream?"

"It's not a dream," said Willa. "It's a party!" She took

Prudence's hand. "And you're the guest of honor. Shall we go inside?"

"Yes . . . Yes!"

Together, they journeyed up the path to the gated mansion, in a scene that seemed to jump right off the pages of Prudence Pock's most frightening fiction. *Just don't count on a happy ending.*

A complete sense of awe had overtaken the more rational contours of Prudence's brain as she and Willa passed through the front foyer of a splendidly spooky estate. There were fancy chandeliers hanging from vaulted ceilings and haunting sonatas playing from unmanned pianos. Again, it was the type of dwelling Prudence Pock often included in her prose. Everywhere she looked, there was something wickedly wondrous to behold. Grinning gargoyles bulged from the walls like beastly boils. There were serpents for door handles. And did we mention the eyes staring from the purple walls?

"What is this place?" asked Prudence. "Why is it here?"

"It began as a retirement home. A spirited retreat, if you will. But over the years, it's evolved into so much more."

Prudence paused by an open doorway. "Is it all right if I take a peek?"

"Be our guest," said Willa. "But no flash pictures, please." The thought hadn't even occurred to Prudence. She was strictly a pen-and-paper girl. She poked her head through the open doorway, peering around the room with her pen-light. It was a portrait chamber. The framed artwork featured ordinary-looking people in vintage clothing: a lady holding a parasol, another with a flower, two gentlemen who could have passed for bankers. "Who are they?" Prudence asked.

"Retirees."

Prudence liked the idea. "You mean, they all live here?"

Willa covered her mouth to hide her giggle. "I wouldn't put it like that. But, yes, you'll find them floating around here somewhere."

And that gave Prudence a thought. "I have a hundred and one Dalmatians—I mean, questions—to ask. Do you think I could have a chat with the owner?"

"The master of tales?" replied Willa in a solemn tone.

Prudence repeated it. "The master of tales." She liked the sound of that, too.

"You'll see him. You'll see everything. Eventually." Together, they left the portrait chamber. Once they were gone, the portraits seemed to . . . *stretch*, the added portions betraying the horrifying fates of their subjects. The lady with the parasol was on a tightrope, about to get munched on by a crocodile. One of the banker types was standing on a barrel of dynamite, the other sitting on the shoulders of two other gents, sinking into quicksand. And the lady with the flower, well, she was sitting on a headstone. Lightning flickered above a domed skylight, adding strobe-like flashes of blue. A cadaverous form swayed from the rafters, its neck twisted in a noose. It was his way out.

In the corridor, organ music seeped through the walls. A funeral dirge. The doors were swelling, as if they were alive and breathing. Prudence was trying to jot it all down, filling up the pages of her notepad with lurid details.

"Your arthritis, it seems to be improving," observed Willa.

Prudence hadn't thought about it. She flexed her fingers. It was true! "Yes, I haven't felt this—" She stopped and stared at Willa. "How did you know about my arthritis?"

"I know all about you, Prudence Pock. Like I said, I'm your biggest fan." Willa drifted off to the next corridor, her angelic form swallowed by gloomy darkness, leaving Prudence to follow the *clink-tink-clink*ing of her charms.

"Where are you taking me?"

Willa's angelic voice came from the shadows. "Don't worry, you'll see. You'll see everything."

They passed a row of picture windows where more lightning was doing some more flashing. The opposite walls were adorned with additional portraits of an uncanny nature: a werecat on a sofa, a gentleman vampire, and a grotesque Gorgon with live snakes for hair, to name a few. "More retirees?" mused Prudence.

"Yes! There are nine hundred ninety-nine of us. With room for a thousand."

A knight in a suit of armor, standing guard at the end of the corridor, drew his sword to point the way. Prudence responded with a deep bow, playing along. "Why, thank you, kind sir. At ease." The knight obliged, removing his helmet . . . along with his entire head! Prudence gushed at the sight. "Marvelous! The effects around here are simply marvelous!" She turned to Willa. "They really should do tours of the place. The public would eat it up!" **And vice versa.**

"This way, Prudence Pock!"

"But I want to stay. I wish to see, to touch, to experience everything this mansion has to offer!"

"Please!" Willa put up her hand in protest. "You must always be careful what you wish for. Now come on. We'll be late for the party."

Willa turned and departed quite suddenly, leaving

Prudence alone. Prudence spun around when she heard Willa call from above.

"Up here!" Prudence saw Willa waving from a balcony and climbed a grand staircase to join her. "Look! The first guests are starting to arrive." Prudence peered down into a grand hall, a large dining room built in another time, seemingly for all time. New arrivals were showing up in horseless hearses from around the globe—Tokyo, Paris, and regions beyond. There were couples waltzing in Victorian garb, the men all wearing gray wigs. It was like a George Washington convention. And for a fleeting moment, Prudence considered that she might be one of them. They only honor you when you're dead, right? *Right?*

But the mere thought of it was patently absurd, for never had Prudence Pock felt so alive. You might even say she felt lighter than air.

Once again, Willa took her by the hand. "Come on! You have to meet my friends." And down they went into the moldering inner sanctum of the grand hall, the nonbeating heart of the festivities.

The first thing Prudence saw was the banquet table. And honestly, you couldn't miss it! It was long enough to accommodate twenty Thanksgivings. Guests were everywhere, and we do mean everywhere—an arm here, a torso there. The invitation had called it a symposium, a gathering of prominent ghost writers. And the guest list did not disappoint. There was Poe, hobnobbing in a corner with Dickens. And Henry James talking shop with Shirley Jackson. Of course, Prudence assumed they were costumed look-alikes. To think otherwise would render her insane. **So what does that make _you_, foolish reader?**

She was elated beyond words, twirling alongside waltzing couples, waving to the phantasms that hung from chandeliers. "This is incredible! I can't believe my eyes!"

Willa took hold of Prudence's hands and twirled along with her. "But you should," she said. "You of all people should believe. You've written about such places your entire natural life."

"Except I know this isn't natural. It isn't a tale. The places, those things I've written about—they were all make-believe. This is . . . is . . . is . . ." Not wanting to sound off her rocker, Prudence let Willa say it for her.

"Real."

"Yes, real."

Prudence stopped twirling. Something was wrong. Reality

was starting to sink in, and she was afraid. Unabashedly afraid. Like Officer Davis afraid. She wanted to leave. To go back to the real world, to her TV and her microwave dinners.

But it was already too late.

She felt an unwelcome distraction. Something flicked her bun. "Stop it! Who's doing that?" It wasn't Poe, and it wasn't Jackson. Who knew? Maybe it was one of the George Washingtons. No! Not any of those.

Prudence heard their impish laughter, and this time she saw them. Three boys, around twelve, were behind her, beaming with excitement. After all, they were big fans, too. Willa smiled as she introduced them. "Prudence Pock, meet my little jerkoids. The rest of the real Gruesome Group—aka the Fearsome Foursome—Tim, Noah, and Steve."

"Thanks for keeping our stories alive," said Tim, the one wearing a baseball uniform.

"I really liked the movie version," added Noah, the chubby one. "Part one. Not so much the other ones."

"That kid they got to play me was lame-lame-lame," chimed in Steve, the handsome one. "And whose dumb idea was it to make Willa a boy?"

"Hey! What's wrong?" Willa asked, seeing the look of horror on Prudence's face.

She was standing inert, petrified as a corpse. **Ah, so there was nothing wrong.** The rational side of her brain had been trying to convince the irrational side that this was all an elaborate put-on. And the rational side had failed. "I need to leave!" she told Willa. "I have a very important appointment in the morning!"

The chilling chimes of a grandfather clock didn't help. The jabbering guests went silent, as silent as the graves they'd crawled out of. It was time for the main event. "What's going on?" Prudence asked in a panic. Willa pointed to the balcony. *Clink-tink-clink.*

The hour of thirteen was upon them, and the master of ceremonies had made his way onto the balcony: a cadaverous figure dressed in the same three-piece suit they'd buried him in, a dead carnation in his lapel. He was the mansion's keeper of tales, Amicus Arcane.

He plucked the flower from his lapel, switching it out for another dead one from a standing vase. He looked down on his beastly brethren. The time had come to announce his retirement.

"Good evening, extinguished and expired guests. Welcome to our grand celebration. For some of you, it was quite a climb.

For others, it was merely a chop, a drip, and a thump. You, dear fiends, have provided tales that have rattled the nerves of the morbid masses. I have collected nine hundred ninety-nine such tales, along with the souls that accompany them. Tonight, we make room for one more." He looked down on the spirited crowd and spotted Prudence standing uncomfortably among them. "My time as your humble librarian has run its unnatural course. All things must pass."

Curiously enough, he was right. A moment later, a *thing* passed.

The guests reacted the way guests do in a haunted mansion; there were shrieks and growls and howls mostly. There might have been a "boo" in there somewhere. Probably from one of the George Washingtons.

The librarian waited for them to settle down before continuing. "Before I depart, however, it is my distinct dishonor to select a beneficiary. The *next* keeper of the tales. The qualifications are maddeningly simple. Tell me a story. Your *scariest* story. Let the contest begin!"

The grand hall erupted with sounds, some defying description, as the ghostly ghost writers began regaling one another with their scariest tales. And as their stories progressed, Prudence noticed sinister transformations occurring throughout the room. She could see right through the floating dancers, peer into the chest cavities of the world's greatest ghost writers, see the glow of their telltale hearts *thump-thump-thump*ing. Prudence understood what was happening, for better or for worse. The mansion was alive—alive with the dead—and Prudence Pock had been invited to join them.

"Aaaaaaaaaaaaahhhhh!"

She unleashed a scream, and some of the guests applauded—the ones with hands, of course.

Prudence bolted for the stairs and only stopped when Willa materialized directly in front of her. "Wait! Where are you going? The party's just getting started."

"I made a mistake, sweetie. This party's not for me!"

"But it is," Willa assured her. "Your final tale needs to be heard."

"Not yet it doesn't!" Prudence ran straight through Willa, going down the up staircase, trying to retrace her path through corridors where doors breathed and walls had eyes, across stairways that defied gravity. She ran through chambers where portraits stretched and masters hung. She moved as fast as her troubled knees could take her, because she could hear them coming. From the darkest recesses of the mansion, a parade of monstrosities was coming to get her.

Those happy haunts she'd heard about—the hitchhikers and the mummies and the brides with hatchets—they had all materialized. And just so we're clear: the haunts are mostly happy because *you're* not! They were almost upon her, and with her writer's block gone, Prudence Pock could vividly imagine what would happen if they caught her!

She made a mad dash for a door—one that wasn't breathing—at the end of the corridor. Its serpent-shaped handle was already turning. Too bad she hadn't noticed. Prudence flew through the door and slammed it behind her.

And instantaneously, the otherworldly noises ceased.

She slowly pivoted, trying to see where she'd ended up. The room had no windows. And when she turned again, she saw that even the door had vanished. It was a quaint chamber, with its overflowing bookshelves, crackling fireplace, and marble busts of the greatest ghost writers the world had ever known. She had stumbled into the mansion's library.

Two female ghosts, one in a white shroud, the other in black, sat in silence in the corner, reading. Upon seeing

Prudence, they nodded, gathered their belongings, and nonchalantly disappeared.

Prudence gulped, then slowly passed the bookshelves, reading titles, hoping deep down to find one or two of her own up there. "Quite the collection, is it not?" She spun around, holding her hand to her heart. A figure was seated in a high-backed chair. She couldn't see his face, but she could guess who he was.

"Mr. Arcane?"

The librarian's skull-like visage creeped out from behind the red velvet; he looked like a worm crawling out of an apple. "Welcome, Mistress Prudence. Welcome to our library. Come. Sit inside the fire. Or is it sit *beside* the fire? I never can get that right."

Prudence nodded, but her legs refused to move. The librarian understood and sent a chair to collect her. It rolled behind Prudence and, after she sat, slid her to the fireplace—where it was oddly chillier. Prudence took a deep breath, gathering all the courage she could muster. It wasn't enough, so she took another breath and gathered some more. "Why am I here, Mr. Arcane? Be honest. Have I gone insane?"

"Hardly," said the librarian. "But hardly's better than

nothing." There was a book in his gloved hands. An old tome with VOLUME IV etched into its spine. He began flipping through the pages—blanks, every one of them. The tales hadn't been written—yet.

"Th-th-there seems to be some misunderstanding," Prudence stammered, her courage fading.

The librarian looked up from the blank pages. "A . . . misunderstanding? Pray tell, elaborate."

"I-I-I don't know that I can. All I know is I don't belong here."

The librarian tilted his head in mock despair. "You *are* the writer Prudence Pock?"

"Y-yes."

"And you *did* receive our invitation?"

She nodded twice. "Yes, yes."

He opened his hands, allowing the book to float onto her lap, then added in a less cordial tone: "Then there is no misunderstanding." Prudence glanced down at the first page and saw her name writing itself in black ink. The librarian offered his most comforting smile, which wasn't very comforting at all. "You have a tale to tell, do you not?"

Prudence slowly nodded, starting to recall. The time had

come for Prudence to regale the librarian with *her* scariest tale of all. **You will hear her terrifying tale soon enough, foolish reader. First, we must return to the asylum. . . .**

Back inside the dungeon of Shepperton Sanitarium, Prudence Pock was holding the same book in her lap. Dr. Ackerman didn't believe a word of what she'd just said and was visually sizing her up for a straitjacket.

"This book, Doctor, it'll make a believer out of you yet."

"It's not what I believe, dear Prudence, it's—"

Their talk was intruded on by a long labored moan, a dispirited plea of gloom. "Cherreeeeeeeee!"

Dr. Ackerman spun around to see where it was coming from. It seemed to be right outside the cell. "What in the world is that?"

"That," said the orderly, reappearing from behind him, "would be the current resident of room three." The orderly readjusted the candelabrum, casting red, yellow, and orange flickers across their faces.

"Cherreeeeeeeee!"

"Would you like to hear *his* tale, Doctor?" Prudence asked.

"And just what do you know of the patient in room three?" Dr. Ackerman replied.

Prudence cracked open the book and flipped through the blank pages, locating the tale she'd been searching for. "Aaah. Here we are, good doctor. The proof is on the page." He leaned in to see. The page was empty except to Prudence Pock. She could see a tale staring back at her. "Indulge me, Doctor. Listen to these . . . tales from the haunted mansion. And then you can determine, once and forever, who is sane and who isn't."

Dr. Ackerman shifted on his stool, trying to conceal his impatience. He couldn't refuse. As a psychiatrist, he had a duty to sit there and listen. "Very well. If you insist, dear Prudence. Let's get on with it."

Prudence Pock unleashed a smile that sent a chill up and down his spine. She turned her eyes to the blank page and began to read.

Interlude

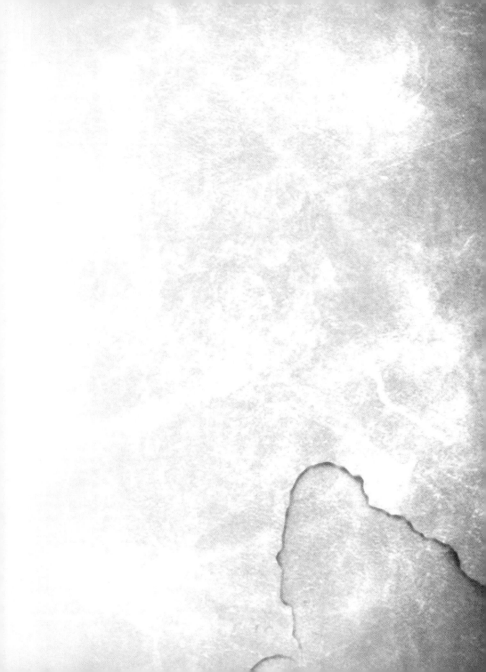

Beware, foolish reader.
Proceed with caution.

The happy haunts have received your
sympathetic vibrations and are
beginning to materialize.

Do you have the guts to join them?

You do?

Very well. Our first tale
happens to be all about guts.

And brains . . .

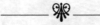

Chapter Three

CLASS BRAIN

"It's alive! Alive!"

And so it was. Alive. Sort of. Juleen, about two seconds away from a full-fledged freak-out, was pointing at the dead-alive thing in the science lab. The frog was attempting to hop, its hind legs kicking with spastic jitters.

Johnson screamed and Corky threw up his mac and cheese lunch, which in turn made Stanley throw up his, which in turn made Madison throw up hers. Soon a squadron of janitors was storming the science lab, armed with mops and buckets of suds to deal with the cheesy mess.

All because a frog decided to do what frogs do naturally.

Sort of. But there was nothing natural during sixth-period science that day. The frog in question had been very dead a few seconds before. Worse than dead, it had been dissected by Shelley, the star science pupil in Mr. Balderston's class. Its internal organs, which had been removed, were on display like so many peas and carrots. The amphibian, Shelley insisted, could be reanimated with a complex electrical charge not seen in nature. She provided the proof by plugging a special surge-amplification cord into her phone, and several zaps later . . . "Rrrr-ribbet!"—a science lesson the students of Buena Vista Middle School would never forget.

Followed by a record-breaking cleanup the janitors of Buena Vista Middle School would never forget.

Mr. Balderston pointed to the exit, too flummoxed to speak. Of course Shelley understood the gesture. She had seen him do it like fifty times before. "You want me to go to the principal and tell him what happened," she said, helping him along, since Mr. Balderston was still unable to form words. The reanimated frog hopped into his shirt pocket. **Don't leave just yet, janitors!** Mr. Balderston promptly joined the puke party. *"Blooo-gah!"* Roast beef on a kaiser roll. *"Blooo-gah!"*—an exact quote, by the way.

Shelley dutifully left the class, the students watching with venomous eyes. So what else was new? Shelley had always been referred to as class brain, and not in a good way. Class brains didn't get asked to dances and always got picked last in gym. "But they sometimes save the world," her grandpapa often said.

Could Shelley help it if she excelled at science? It was in her DNA. She hailed from a not-so-distinguished line of scientists dating back to medieval times—the type who performed their experiments in Gothic towers. A few of her relations had even been burned at the stake for being witches. Thank goodness Shelley lived in enlightened times. These days, punishment for mad scientists amounted to a trip to the principal's office.

Sitting across from Mr. Gribbons, Shelley questioned her latest infraction. "I don't understand. What did I do wrong?"

Mr. Gribbons was just as flummoxed as Shelley's teacher. That happened when a student cornered him with logic. "What you did . . ." he started. Then he stopped, looking around for an assist from elsewhere. A plaque on his desk caught his eye. It said HONESTY ISN'T THE BEST POLICY—IT'S THE ONLY POLICY! That helped. Sort of. "What you did," he said, rearranging the plaque, "it was dishonest."

"How so?"

"You say you brought a dead thing back to life. That's impossible, Shelley. It implies you performed a miracle."

Shelley looked down at her timid hands. They weren't the hands of a god. They were the hands of a kid who got picked last in gym. But when he said it out loud, it sounded like she'd done a bad thing. Science wasn't bad and it wasn't good. It just *was*. Real science was never a lie. So she responded with the truth. "It wasn't a trick, Mr. Gribbons. Or a miracle. It was science. Go down to the lab and see for yourself." She spared him the details about the frog's insides being on the outside.

But it seemed honesty wasn't Mr. Gribbons's only policy, and Shelley was rewarded with a two-day suspension.

Shelley had plenty of time to think about it during the long walk home. She shuffled along the sidewalk, stepping on the cracks she wished could break her mother's back. Not literally. The idea had nothing to do with her actual mother. It would just be nice if she could believe in something that wasn't science. Why couldn't she be like the other kids, who grew up believing in tooth fairies and leprechauns? Why couldn't she laugh at the jokes the boys told at recess? Simple. Because the jokes weren't funny. But that didn't stop the other girls from laughing, in their cute outfits, not frumpy dresses handmade by their moms. She wished she could believe in the magic of sunsets and waterfalls, but really, there wasn't anything to believe. They weren't magic. They just *were*.

But more than that, Shelley wished she could believe in love.

She would have traded all fourteen science fair ribbons for that. Or just a friend, any friend. Science wasn't Shelley's friend. It was a fact. And facts, as good as they were, were loveless and cold. As cold as the grave.

Shelley heard a buzz coming at her from behind. It was probably a fat bumblebee, looking to add a stinging exclamation point to Shelley's already crummy day. She turned and saw a red bike heading straight for her, the buzz emanating from baseball cards attached to the spokes. She quickly jumped out of the way and found herself getting doused by a sprinkler on someone's lawn.

The bike came to a stop and a stranger stepped off: a tallish boy, his face obscured by stringy black bangs. Shelley thought about booking it out of there, but there was a reason she got picked last in gym. Booking wasn't her thing. As he moved toward her, Shelley tried scaring him off. "Stand back! I'm a master of tofu!"

The boy brushed the hair from his face. And what a face it was. It belonged to Hank Clerval, a kid Shelley knew from grade school. More than knew. For a while, they had been inseparable. But that was in the good old days, before a terrible tragedy struck Hank's family. His older brother had been killed in an accident. Shelley remembered seeing his picture on the cover of the town flyer, and then Hank was out of school for what seemed like forever. When he finally did come back, he was different. Like he was no longer Hank. At least, no longer the Hank she knew. They'd been no more than cordial ever since. Shelley never spoke about her feelings, not to her mom or her grandpapa. Perhaps she even tried hiding them from herself. But not having Hank Clerval in her world had broken her heart.

Now he was standing across from her and Shelley had to look away. She was soaked and humiliated. She expected him to laugh, but he didn't—truly a miracle. "Hey, Shellfish, long time no see."

He remembers, she thought. Hank had given her that nickname, back when Hank was still Hank.

He lowered his kickstand and hopped off the bike. "You might want to move away from that sprinkler."

Shelley chuckled nervously. "Just cooling off. It's hot, isn't it? Are you hot? I'm hot." He smiled, and all the old feelings flooded back to her. It was a smile she remembered, except now it didn't have braces. It had perfect teeth.

"Yeah, now that you mention it, I'm boiling," he responded, and joined her under the sprinkler, where they got soaked together. It was the first time she and Hank had laughed since the fourth grade.

Minutes later, they were walking side by side down the street. "I heard a crazy rumor today," Hank said. "Some dude said you brought a dead frog back to life in science."

Shelley's heart sank. At that moment, the last thing she wanted to be was the class brain. "It wasn't really dead," she explained. "It was just resting, waiting for a new life to come." *That came out weird,* she thought, and she fully expected him to make a mad escape, just like every other boy she knew. But he didn't.

"I believe you."

"You do?"

"Yes, I do. More than that, I believe *in* you." He extended his hand. "Will you come home with me? I'd like you to meet someone. I live just over the hill." He pointed to a large blue house that peeked out from the other side of the hill; it was the one with a wraparound porch that Shelley often admired on the days she got sent home early—which happened a lot.

Don't judge a book—or a house—by its cover, Mistress Shelley. Or a mansion.

Hank unlocked the front door and led Shelley into the den. "Mom, we have company!" The inside of the house was a perfect match for the outside: neat and tidy, everything in order, each knickknack properly placed. Shelley couldn't believe people actually lived that way. The sofa matched the curtains, and the wallpaper matched the sofa, and they all matched the ottoman. It was almost *too* perfect. Was there such a thing as too perfect?

The amazing smell coming from the kitchen signaled that there were cookies, too. Fresh out of the oven!

A sprightly woman wearing an apron that matched the curtains—which meant it matched the ottoman—sprinted in from the kitchen, carrying a plate of freshly baked chocolate chip cookies. How fresh? Try *steam rising, chips melting* fresh. "Would you like one?" she asked.

Shelley selected the smallest cookie out of politeness. "Thank you, Mrs. Clerval."

Mrs. Clerval smiled, recognizing her. "Shelley, isn't it? I remember you from the science fair. There's quite a brain floating around in that skull." Shelley thanked her. But why did it always have to be about her brain? "Your theory on electrogalvanism as it pertains to the reanimation of dead tissue was the highlight of the fair. I was upset when the papier-mâché volcano took the top prize."

"What can you do?" Shelley shrugged, smiling uncomfortably. "Who ever said life was fair?" She bit into the cookie and immediately thought to spit it out. Not in front of Hank, of course. It didn't taste very good. In fact, it tasted fake. Like the Clervals themselves, the cookie looked too good to be true.

"Please. Have another."

"No thank you. I've got dinner waiting at home."

"Shelley performed some sort of miracle today. You really need to hear this, Mom."

Shelley smiled shyly. "Yeah, it's a miracle I only got two days of suspension instead of three."

But Hank wasn't smiling. "She brought a dead amphibian back to life," he said, and his mother let out a squeal, dropping the plate of cookies all over the carpet. It was an uncomfortable moment. Shelley got down on her knees and began gathering them up.

"Leave those!" shouted Mrs. Clerval. "You're not a maid, you're a scientist. Yes, I know all about your family, their famous discoveries. And the indignities they suffered for them. You, dear Shelley, will carry on in their grand tradition." A mask had been removed and the real Mrs. Clerval had been revealed. She wasn't a woman who spent her afternoons dusting shelves and baking cookies.

Shelley knew it was time to hightail it out of there. "I, um, have to get home. My grandpapa's expecting me any minute. In fact, I'm late already."

"Please, we won't keep you long. There's still time," said Mrs. Clerval.

"Time? For what?" asked Shelley.

Mrs. Clerval took Shelley by the hand and helped her to her feet. "Time to meet the rest of my family."

Mrs. Clerval led Shelley down a long metal staircase into the dark regions of the prettiest house in the neighborhood. *Oh, if only all houses could be judged by their outsides.* Deep, deep into the subbasement they descended. Shelley could feel the temperature changing the lower they got. And a smell, the stench of electric fumes, had infiltrated her nostrils. Not the damp, mildewy smell one normally associated with a basement under a basement.

"Hank, throw the switch!" Mrs. Clerval ordered. There was a small lever protruding from a stone wall. Hank yanked it down, and everywhere lights burst into being. At once, Shelley understood why they'd brought her below. Hidden beneath this handsome house was the laboratory of Shelley's dreams! Because, well, people like Shelley dreamed of laboratories. The lab was loaded with exotic tools—some she could identify, others she could not. There were beakers boiling over with potions, red, yellow, and green, and electrical equipment stacked on top of computers.

"What do you think?" asked Hank.

"What do I think?" Shelley made it down the last two steps on her own, twirling to take it all in. "I think it's incredible! That's a Tesla coil over there! And over there—is that a megavolt regulator?" But the lab wasn't the only thing they wanted her to see.

Shelley stopped breathing when the main attraction came into view. Stretched out along a large metal table, covered by a sheet that matched the ottoman, was the hideous phantasm of a man. Mrs. Clerval made the formal introduction.

"Shelley, I'd like you to meet my son." Hank rolled away the sheet, and Shelley unleashed a most unscientific scream. "This is Adam."

The body on the slab was unusually tall, at least seven feet; it was an unhealthy bluish green, and the appendages didn't quite match up. One arm was slightly longer than the other. The ears had dissimilar shapes. The legs were the same size, but the knees bent in different places. And with the eyes closed, he looked more asleep than dead.

Mrs. Clerval latched on to Shelley's arm, pulling her in close, inviting her to examine the fine details of a body meticulously stitched together like a quilt from mismatched parts.

"How long has he been dead?" Shelley managed to ask.

"Not dead," replied Mrs. Clerval.

Hank added, "He's just resting. Waiting for a new life to come."

Mrs. Clerval explained that she had failed in numerous attempts to endow the body with life. And what a chore it had become keeping the parts from going the natural route— that is to say *from rotting*.

"He looks pretty fresh to me," said Shelley. That was the closest she could get to a compliment.

"It's been a challenge," said Mrs. Clerval. "We're constantly disposing of old parts, replacing them with . . . new ones."

"Replacing them. From where?" *Hint, hint, Mistress Shelley: They come in oblong boxes six feet under the ground. Don't forget your shovel. Heh!*

"Does it matter where they came from? What matters is how well they work." Shelley saw an empty jar labeled *Adam's brain* on a nearby counter. She felt her own mac and cheese lunch wriggling its way up through her pipes. Seeing no signs of a janitor, Shelley politely swallowed.

"Whatever you do in the privacy of your own home is your own business," she said, uttering a sentiment she'd heard her grandpapa express. And it seemed like a good line to depart on. So Shelley bolted for the stairs.

"Shellfish! Please don't leave!" Hank implored her. "We need your help."

She paused on the middle step. "My help? I don't understand."

Hank covered the body while his mother approached the stairs. "You have the scientific means," he said. "It's in your blood. You can bring my brother back to life."

Shelley wasn't sure what to say. True, the very thought was somewhat exciting. If Shelley could pull something like that off, she'd be more than a class brain—she'd be a world brain! She might even clear the disgraced family name once and for all. The question was, did she have the right? Bringing back a dead frog was one thing. But a dead human being?

A crackle of thunder seemed to respond. A storm was in the forecast, but Shelley took it as a sign. The thunder was an admonishment from God.

Chapter Four

CLASS BRAIN (PART 2)

Being needed for something other than her science homework would be a new experience for Shelley. She'd always dreamed about being needed by someone for anything. "Would you go to the dance with me, Shelley?" would be nice. "Would you share an acai bowl with me, Shelley?"—even nicer. But "Would you bring a dead body back to life for me, Shelley?"—that was typical.

She was the weird girl. The class brain, then and always. Maybe it was time to accept it. Some of the other weird kids had. And as her grandpapa often said, it was good to be known for something. Reanimating dead things—that was *something*. As an experiment, it pounded those papier-mâché volcanoes into the ground. But this—this request went beyond even class brain limits. Admittedly, she'd already brought a croaked frog back to croaking life, but that was small potatoes compared to this. Bringing back a dead person was repellent. Maybe even illegal. Forget a two-day suspension. She'd be suspended for life! *If bringing back the dead is wrong, I don't want to be right.*

"I'm sorry. I couldn't do it even if I wanted to," she informed the Clervals. But saying it was so much harder than she'd imagined. Shelley saw hope drain from Mrs. Clerval's eyes. It was like watching a mother lose her child for the second time.

During the first day of Shelley's suspension, all she could think about was Mrs. Clerval's shattered expression. The repeated inquiries: "Why, Shelley? Why? Why?" The disappointment shared by Hank. And then she pictured a joyous family reunion, the happy tears that would flow if Adam came back into their world. It would be better than a blue ribbon. That would be the science project to end all science projects.

But did she have the right?

On the second day of her suspension, Shelley began redoing the calculations on her laptop. Multiplying. Reconfiguring. She soon realized that, technically, the experiment would be a logical extension of her grandpapa's electrophysiological theories. The same spark used to resurrect a dead frog could reanimate a human body. If she increased power to the poles, the heart would recharge. It would be like galvanizing a dormant battery. Sort of.

If only she'd been to school the past two days. The talk was all about the frog: how it had gone berserk, biting Mr. Gribbons before making its escape into the schoolyard. A posse of janitors with torches and pitchforks was sent out to find it. **Don't ask. It's an angry-mob thing.** By then, Mr. Balderston was no longer referring to it as a frog.

He was calling it a monster.

Another week passed before Shelley ran into Hank on her walk home. He apologized, asking her to forget everything she had seen in the lab. It would be pretty hard to forget seeing a cadaver on a slab, but she told him she would try. "Thank you, Shelley. I always knew you were special." He gave her an unexpected peck on the cheek, and Shelley thought, *He's a lost soul. Just like me.* And wasn't he a lost soul worth finding?

Just as they were about to go their separate ways, Shelley shouted, "I want to help!" though she wasn't sure she really did.

That afternoon, as Shelley and Hank shared an overpriced acai bowl at World o' Coffee, Shelley told Hank what she'd been thinking about. "I think I can pull it off. But, Hank, I want you to understand: there's no guarantee it's going to work. Your brother isn't a frog."

"It'll work," he said with certainty. "It's science!"

"Yes, it is. But since seeing you again, I've been thinking about more than just science. I've been thinking about fate. About souls."

Hank stared at her for a long moment. "Go on," he said, clearly unsure of where the conversation was headed.

"That cadaver, the one you call your brother—does it have a soul? Do you think its spirit is at rest?"

"Sure, I guess."

"Then what if it doesn't want to be woken up? He's been gone for so long. It may be too late."

Hank squirmed uncomfortably in the booth. "I'm not an expert on ghosts." *I concur.* "All I know is that you've been given a gift—and your family is good at weird science. Don't you think it's about time you embraced who you are?"

Shelley sat back and thought about it. She was the weird girl. The class brain. It was good to be known for something, right?

Hank took her hands and looked directly into her eyes. "You're the only one who can help." Overwhelmed with emotion, Shelley returned his gaze and said with confidence, "All right. Let's do this."

Hank leaned across the table and kissed her—on the lips!—right over the acai bowl. "Come on. Let's go tell my mother!"

"Okay!" Shelley replied, her face as red as his bicycle.

It felt like she was flying! Shelley was on the handlebars of Hank's bike, gliding toward the nicest house in the neighborhood: the one with a mad scientist's lab in the subbasement. They hadn't held hands since the fourth grade, let alone shared an acai bowl. But in her recent flights of fantasy, which had little place for actual science, save biology, Shelley came to the conclusion that she had always been in love with Hank. And she still was.

The future "Mr. Shelley."

As they approached the bottom of the hill that led to the blue house, Hank slowed down and Shelley hopped off the handlebars. "Where are you going?" he asked.

"Home," she said. "I have to ask grandpapa a few things. And you, Hank Clerval, need to talk to your mom in private. It's a family thing."

Hank smiled warmly. "You are family."

They exchanged last smiles, and she watched him ride off, his red bicycle disappearing over the hill. And quite suddenly, Shelley felt an ache she could not identify. She had always admired Hank from afar. Now she couldn't imagine a world without him. Well, it didn't matter what she could imagine. Fate was about to lend a cruel hand.

Shelley heard the terrible screech of tires. And then there was a sickening thud.

She ran up the hill, hoping not to see her worst fear become a reality. People were already gathering around the scene of an accident, pointing fingers, identifying the victim. "It's Hank! Hank Clerval! He's been run over by a car!"

The door to the blue house flew open and Hank's mother emerged onto the porch. She saw a body and flashing lights in the street as another one of her sons lay dying.

Shelley ran to Hank's side and checked his vitals. Mrs.

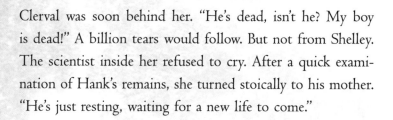

Clerval was soon behind her. "He's dead, isn't he? My boy is dead!" A billion tears would follow. But not from Shelley. The scientist inside her refused to cry. After a quick examination of Hank's remains, she turned stoically to his mother. "He's just resting, waiting for a new life to come."

Shelley had to work quickly. The only way to really save Hank was to use Adam's body. Mrs. Clerval agreed.

The details of how Hank's brain wound up floating in a glass jar might be a bit much for certain readers (foolish or otherwise) but that's never stopped us before. To simplify, let's just say that it involved a bone saw grinding through his skull, that the brain itself was removed from the cranium like a large oyster and plopped into an alcohol-based solution to prevent it from turning to mush. But we'll spare you the gory details. Let's just say Hank's brain was floating in a glass jar.

Hank's body, on the other hand, had been unreasonably mangled in the accident. Those details might be a bit too graphic for certain readers, so again, we'll simplify. To start with, his left leg wound up where his . . . Oh, never mind. Hank's body was too damaged to reanimate. So with Mrs. Clerval's approval, Shelly began collecting spare parts from local graveyards. **And now you know why we keep ours locked.**

Hank's brain was subsequently placed inside the skull of a newly retooled body. That would be the reconstructed cadaver on the slab. The operation to give the body life was scheduled for a long holiday weekend, since Shelley had already missed too much school. For Mrs. Clerval, it was like killing two birds with one lightning bolt. If the experiment proved successful, she'd be reunited with both her sons.

For Shelley, it was another chance at Hank.

Sort of.

That Saturday night, while most of her classmates were at the movies or playing miniature golf, Shelley was holed up in the Clervals' laboratory, knee-deep in body parts. All the last-minute preparations had been made. The equipment was ready, and a massive electrical storm was on its way. Mrs. Clerval had been relegated to assistant status. Shelley's Ygor, if you will. When Shelley said, "Throw the switches!" Mrs. Clerval threw the switches.

Hank's brain had already been inserted into Adam's skull. An antenna had been attached to the roof, camouflaged as a satellite dish, drawing in the required spark of life. Machines whirled and beakers shook. There were blue flashes of electricity and showers of sparks.

Stitched together from disparate parts, the large cadaver on the slab was starting to glow. The power surged directly through small metal bolts inserted into the temples. The body was recharging, the legs twitching like Shelley's frog. Shelley and her assistant, Hank's mom, watched in awe as the larger of the two hands seemed to form a fist. Was Hank . . . ?

"Alive?" Mrs. Clerval asked. "Is he alive?"

Shelley began spinning knobs to decrease the current. Thin wisps of smoke snaked up from the cadaver's eyes, ears, and nose. Shelley yelled for Mrs. Clerval to switch off the generator, fearing the body might burst into flames. Fortunately, it didn't.

Mrs. Clerval watched with her heart in her mouth (ahh, the lunch special) as Shelley placed a stethoscope on the cadaver's chest, hoping the spirit of Hank had returned to the body she was trying to reanimate. But Shelley heard nothing. She put her cheek to his lips. Again, there was nothing. Not even a puff of air. She turned to Mrs. Clerval. "I'm so sorry."

The science experiment to end all science experiments had failed.

The experiment—and its failure—had taken a great toll on Shelley. An entire month later, she still couldn't kick it. Not to mention it was a gym day. But then something happened during homeroom that turned it all around. Call it a miracle if you want. *Go ahead, I'll wait.*

Mr. Sangster had just announced the arrival of a new student. He didn't say where the student was from, but Shelley almost had a heart attack when she saw him—all seven-plus feet of him! "Let's all give a big Buena Vista Middle School welcome to . . . Adam!"

A hulking figure backed into the classroom, barely fitting through the door. Turning slowly, he made a dramatic reveal to the class. Shelley heard a triple thud, later identified as the sound of three kids fainting.

The new student had a slightly bluish-green complexion; his eyes were sunken, and his pupils were a sickly yellow. His parts seemed not to match—one arm a little longer, one leg a little shorter—yet the mad stitchwork went unmentioned. He was just a little too menacing to make fun of.

Shelley would later learn that the cadaver had woken up less than twenty-four hours after she had left the lab. Mrs. Clerval had kept his reanimation a secret and, for the next month, had nursed him to his current state. That would be *direct current, as in one hundred thousand volts.*

The boy lumbered clumsily toward an empty desk, his

coordination not yet there. It was the desk behind Shelley. He sat, barely able to squeeze his mismatched parts into the chair, and Shelley turned to face him. His bluish lips formed a smile. Somehow, he recognized her. Deep within the recesses of a mushy brain that used to be Hank's, in a body that had started out as Adam's, the creature recognized Shelley.

"Hank, are you in there?" Shelley asked.

"His name is Adam," Mr. Sangster said, sternly correcting her. "He's new."

"Of course," said Shelley.

It was crazy how things sometimes worked out. Class brain one day, class sweetheart the next. You see, in the semester that followed, Shelley had herself a not-so-secret admirer. The Adam-Hank hybrid followed her everywhere, clinging to her like a lost puppy. Or perhaps a lost soul. They sat together at lunch, the only two at their table—or forty-two, if you counted the parts that had gone into creating him. Shelley taught "Adam" rudimentary words, like *friend* and *good*. Also, having a seven-plus-foot-tall creature on your team provided certain advantages at gym. For the first time, she was the last one standing in dodgeball. The creature had decimated the opposing team with line drive shots, sending the more obnoxious players limping into the nurse's office.

In the following weeks, Shelley and the creature did all the things you see couples doing in those syrupy movie montages: picnicking by a lake, flying kites, eating ice cream. And their first kiss in the gazebo was electric—literally! Of course, they also did some things you don't see couples doing in those movie montages, like replacing worn-out body parts and sewing up gnarly limbs.

Unfortunately, the mushy remains of the complex computer known as Hank's brain no longer functioned the way it was supposed to. True, the hybrid creature loved his Shelley, but without Hank's precise memories, he simply didn't know why. Yet his feelings were more than bluish-green-skin-deep. His was a passion that had survived death and transcended bodies.

But all things must pass.

Their love story, one of the strangest ever told, was doomed from the very first spark.

The tragic ending began on the night of the middle school dance, the first and only one Shelley attended. She and "Adam" were doing the chicken dance in the middle of the gym when a bully shoved into them. "Watch it, freak!"

The remark didn't sit well with the creature. And when the bully insulted Shelley directly, making fun of the dress her mom had made, the creature took matters into his own, mismatched hands. The bully was sent sailing like a dodgeball into a punch bowl. Fruit juice splashed everything and everyone. There was shoving and shouting, and before anyone knew it, the dance had turned into a disaster. The staff soon had a full-blown riot on their hands, and not a laugh riot! Principal Gribbons was already looking for someone to pin it on.

The bully in the punch bowl pointed at Shelley. "It was her! She started it! That freak and her freak boy-thing!"

Gribbons nodded. "Shelley." *Of course. Who else could it be?*

Shelley took the creature by his unusually large hand. "I need to get you out of here!" They pushed their way through the crowd, making it to a back exit. The door was locked, but that really wasn't a problem. The creature gave it a shove and it flew off the hinges. Then they went into the schoolyard, where Hank's red bicycle was waiting, chained to a bike rack. The creature bypassed the lock, shredding the chain like string cheese. By then the mob of students, teachers, and chaperones was piling out of the gym, screaming for justice. Some of them were carrying torches. **Again, it's an angry-mob thing. They came prepared.**

Shelley was driving the bike, with the uncoordinated creature relegated to the handlebars. She pumped as hard as she could, but the mob was right behind them, gaining fast.

The bike had made it halfway up the hill, just out of range of the pretty blue house, when Shelley's legs gave out. "I can't pedal anymore," she told the creature. "My legs are on fire."

He growled. "Fire no good!"

The bike started rolling backward, down the hill, where the angry mob was making its ascent. Shelley took out her cell. "I'm calling your mom for help!" She phoned Mrs. Clerval and told her the situation. Mrs. Clerval said she'd be there in a minute.

But the angry mob would be there in less than a minute. Orange torchlight had made its way onto the hill, along with irate voices: "There it is! It's a monster! Kill the monster!"

The creature looked at Shelley and his bilious eyes formed tears—the biggest tears she had ever seen. "Go!" he cried. "You live!" And he leaped off the handlebars.

"What are you doing? Get back on the bike!"

The creature shook his head. "Go!"

"Not without you!"

"Yes! You live!"

She gazed into his eyes a final time and saw the creature's soul. It was Hank's spirit, now trapped in Adam's makeshift body. And she told them both, "I love you."

The creature gave the bike a monstrous shove, and Shelley went flying, straight over the hill and out of sight. Adam's mismatched mouth formed a gargantuan grin. Even as the angry mob surrounded him, preparing to tear him limb from limb, Adam smiled, knowing she had gotten away.

Fueled by blind hatred, the mob began to chant: "Destroy! Destroy! Destroy!"

But the creature was not destroyed, and the mob stopped chanting when they heard the screeching tires, followed by a thud. And then came the panicked voices from the other side of the hill. "It's the weird girl! The class brain! She's been hit! Somebody call an ambulance!"

The creature forced his way through the crowd, knocking down villagers like dominoes. He lurched awkwardly up the hill and only slowed when he saw the red bike under the car. Shelley's body was lying next to it. The creature staggered over and dropped to his mismatched knees.

The driver got out of the car. It was Mrs. Clerval, who'd been speeding over to help. She looked into the eyes of her boy as he knelt protectively over Shelley's body. Then he unleashed a pitiful moan from the very depths of his godless soul that would not cease for as long as his reanimated heart remained beating. Mrs. Clerval understood the profoundness of his pain. She understood it as only a mother could. For the creature wasn't a being of thought. He was a being of emotion. One born of love.

Some considered it justice. Some said Shelley paid the ultimate price for stepping on God's toes. Others insisted her death was the result of blind hatred, the hatred of those who would hunt and destroy anything they didn't understand.

As for the creature . . . he was sent to the dungeon of Shepperton Sanitarium, where his piteous moans can still be heard, night after night after night.

"Cherreeeeeeeee!"

Chapter Five

WHAT DO YOU BELIEVE?

❧

Prudence Pock looked up from the book to find Dr. Ackerman staring, his mouth agape, not at her, necessarily, but at the final page of the tale he'd just heard. "May I see that?"

"Of course, Doctor." She passed him the book, and his jaw dropped even farther. The words were all there. The entire story had somehow materialized.

"That's quite a trick."

"I'm here all week," she said, adding some levity. She glanced at the rectangular slot. The eyes of the orderly were there, always watching. This time, she thought she heard him muffle a small laugh. The doctor was not amused. He returned the book, his wonderment becoming resentment. The doctor didn't like being made a fool of, especially by "one of them."

"Your thoughts, Doctor?"

"My thoughts, dear Prudence, are inconsequential. But if you're asking for my literary evaluation . . ."

Prudence leaned forward, close enough for him to feel her breath. It was cold—as cold as the dungeon. "Don't be so stuffy. I'm asking if you liked it. Was it . . . believable? The story you just heard. Do you think it really happened?"

Dr. Ackerman said nothing at first. He had to weigh his words. He didn't believe in an afterlife; therefore, as a by-product, he did not believe in ghost stories. But that didn't mean he didn't enjoy them. He enjoyed them immensely, actually—a fact he hoped to keep hidden from Prudence Pock for as long as he could. You see, Dr. Ackerman loved a good scare as much as anyone. You might even say he was an expert. *Go ahead, say it.*

"Interesting. I'd say it's more sorrowful than scary. But not terribly convincing. I mean, who'd believe such a tale? It's outlandish."

"It's Adam," she replied.

Prudence began incessantly tapping the book cover with her nails. *Tap, tap, tap.* Dr. Ackerman found it grating. *This is why we put them in straitjackets,* he thought. Prudence Pock was waiting for his real answer. *Tap, tap, tap.* Like the mansion itself, she demanded one. *Tap, tap, tap.*

Dr. Ackerman cleared his throat. "As a story, I suppose it had its share of unsettling moments. But if we're being honest, all that gore . . . it isn't my thing."

"That's not what I asked, as you well know. I asked if you believed. A simple yes or no, Doctor. You either do or you don't."

The doctor had to tread lightly. The wrong answer could send a seemingly docile patient into a rage. It was best just to pacify her. "I believe that you believe. Is that enough of an affirmation?"

"No, it is not!" Prudence sprang from her stool, and Dr. Ackerman reflexively sprang from his, backing into the padded wall. Pointing her finger, Prudence raged: "That tale was not born of my brain! It came from a resident! It was *her* tale."

"A resident of the mansion?"

Prudence quickly settled down. "Yes, Dr. Ackerman."

"And this resident . . . does she have a name?"

All at once, an inhuman wail perforated the walls. "Cherreeeeeeeee!" It sounded like an animal in mourning.

"He's been calling her name this entire time, good doctor."

"You—you think he's been calling Shelley?" Prudence nodded, and the hairs on the back of Dr. Ackerman's neck stood on end. But the doctor wouldn't give in, wouldn't relent. "But this unfortunate creature, this Adam, as you call him—how did he relay such a tale? You painted him as a near mute. Barely articulate."

"And he still is." Prudence Pock was smiling again. "You're not listening, Doctor; that tale didn't come from Adam. It came from Shelley herself. She's just one of the nine hundred ninety-nine happy haunts who have retired to the mansion."

The doctor placed his hand over the page, cutting her off. "Right. Your supposed haunted mansion. Tell me more about this phantom manor of yours. You've established how you got in. The cryptic invitation. The horseless carriage. But I'm wondering how you got out."

Prudence unleashed a wide all-knowing grin that would make Amicus Arcane envious. "Maybe I didn't get out. Maybe I'm still inside. Both of us, Doctor, trapped within its corridors. Entombed for all eternity." She added a raspy chortle

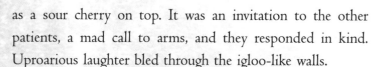

as a sour cherry on top. It was an invitation to the other patients, a mad call to arms, and they responded in kind. Uproarious laughter bled through the igloo-like walls.

Naturally, proclaiming himself sane, Dr. Ackerman wasn't in on the joke. But to the residents of the dungeon, he was the joke. Disbelief in an afterlife—denial of a universe beyond what we can smell and touch and see—was the ultimate punch line to those who'd been there. There would be terrible consequences for some, dark delicacies for others. It all depended on what one's soul brought to the party.

Dr. Ackerman left room 4, trying to process what he'd just been told. The tale was nonsense, of course. *Outlandish* was the word he had used. In his professional opinion, Prudence Pock was insane. The wall between rational reality and frightening fiction had collapsed. That was why they'd brought her to Shepperton in the first place. But certain aspects of the story resonated, and Dr. Ackerman found himself, perhaps subconsciously, feeling his way through the corridor, searching for room 3, his eyes probing the suddenly dark hallway.

Had something changed? Was it the deprived lighting? Because the corridor now looked both narrow and endless.

The pitiful wail grew louder. "Cherreeeeeeeee!" The

mournful cry came again, even louder this time. "Cherree-eeeeeee!" Dr. Ackerman took another step toward it when . . .

A gloved hand clamped down on his shoulder, and the doctor almost died from fright. The orderly was behind him, holding his candelabrum. "Aaah, there you are, Doctor. I thought we'd lost you to the shadows. Have you extracted all you required from the patient?"

"No, we're not finished. I just needed a little air."

"Yes, it can be a bit stuffy in here. As stuffy as a tomb."

The remark struck a nerve. "A tomb. That's what she implied while discussing this mysterious mansion."

"Mysterious, sir?"

"All right. Haunted, then!"

The orderly nodded. "We had an expert here once. A scientist who claimed to know all about it. This *haunted mansion*, as you call it."

Dr. Ackerman perked up, his expression curious. "Who was this so-called expert? And where is he now?"

The orderly shifted the candelabrum so only his head was illuminated. In the flickering light, that looked different, too. Like the corridor itself, his face appeared to narrow, resembling a skull. "I'll answer the second part first. The so-called expert is currently deceased."

"Currently?"

"Gone on to a better place. Or is it a *deader* place? I never can get that right."

Dr. Ackerman grew impatient. "We'd all like to believe. But we mustn't allow childhood fantasies to interfere with cold, hard reality."

"What *is* cold, hard reality, Doctor?"

"Simply put: dead is dead!"

"That's *your* opinion," said the orderly. "However, getting back to our expert . . ."

"So-called."

"The gentleman's name was Rand Brisbane."

The doctor hesitated. "I know the name. He was a medium or a mind reader or something."

"Master Rand was the leading authority on those realities you deem childish. He claimed to have been inside the mansion, to have spent an entire evening amongst its inhabitants."

"A claim he made after he was brought here?"

"That is correct, good doctor."

"A claim made from within the walls of a madhouse. With due respect, Mr. Coats, it's not a very convincing argument. I expect such musings from some of my patients. But this? It's pure fantasyland." *Not to be confused with Tomorrowland or Adventureland or Frontierland . . .*

Their talk was intruded upon by that long, labored moan, a cry of infinite sadness. "Cherreeeeeeeee!" Dr. Ackerman turned to face the orderly, eager to see his reaction to the sound. Coats readjusted the candelabrum, casting red, yellow, and orange flickers on the next door.

Dr. Ackerman cautiously approached the rectangular slot. The glass had veins snaking through it, as if it had been smashed. "I can't make out a thing. Where's the patient?" He spotted a lumpy shape on the floor: a pile of torn rags Dr. Ackerman recognized. "His straitjacket. It's been torn to shreds!"

The orderly nodded. "Patient three dislikes being confined."

"But that's impossible! You can't tear out of a straitjacket. It would require inhuman strength!"

"Aptly put," said the orderly. "Aptly put."

"Cherreeeeeeeee!"

This time, the moan was accompanied by a face, jolting into the rectangular slot. Dr. Ackerman lurched back, startled. He didn't get a good look at the unfortunate creature, but he saw its bilious eyes darting to and fro. Sorrowful eyes, rendering its guttural pleas more pitiful than petrifying.

"Cherreeeeeeeee!" The very walls vibrated.

Dr. Ackerman aimed his cell light through the rectangular slot and located the hulking silhouette of a man; the poor soul was on its knees. The incongruous parts, the slightly bluish-green complexion: everything matched the description in Prudence's tale. "Cherreeeeeeeee! Cherreeeeeeeee!"

And it hit Dr. Ackerman: "By God, it's true."

Dr. Ackerman returned to room 4 and stood in the doorway, staring at Prudence Pock. Neither spoke; neither moved. The silent standoff lasted for what seemed like an eternity. Then, without a word, Prudence curled her lips in a wide sinister grin and lifted volume four.

The doctor entered, then watched as Prudence opened the book and silently sifted through blank pages until she found what she was looking for. "X marks the rot," she said. "This tale involves a hidden treasure, one that should have stayed hidden—like a lot of things in this world, Doctor. And the next. Some things are supposed to remain buried."

Alert, the doctor leaned in close, listening. Yes, he wanted to hear it. As much as Prudence Pock wanted to tell it. As much as the spirits it involved wanted it told. Thanks to the foreboding nature of his curious profession, Dr. Ackerman had become the perfect audience for her spirited tales. *Just like you, foolish reader.*

Prudence looked down at the page and began to read aloud the words that weren't there.

Interlude

Aah, there you are!
Our ghosts have been dying to meet you.

We spirits haunt our best
in gloomy darkness.

So turn out the lights
and look alive!
(For as long as you can.)

A spiteful spirit from centuries past
has perilous plans for you, foolish matey.

Snip-snip!

———— ✖ ————

Chapter Six

A PIRATE'S DEATH FOR ME

The old lighthouse keeper loved giving middle school tours. He'd been doing them for half a century.

Visitors came to Displeasure Island for the pretty views and fine dining. But mostly they came to see the lighthouse, because it was extraordinary. Not so much in its duties. If we're being honest, it did what most lighthouses do. But in life *(and the afterlife)* it's all about appearances. The Displeasure Island lighthouse was built in the likeness of a pirate—a 168-foot-tall pirate.

And the man who looked after it was also the keeper of its tales. For fifty years, the old lighthouse keeper had entertained the visiting middle schoolers with stories of Captain Gore and his bloody band of pirates. The kids who gathered around him now were enraptured by his finely honed skills as a raconteur. Well, most of them. There was that one obnoxious kid in the back. We'll get to him in a minute. For now, let's listen in.

"Ahoy, foolish mateys! Gather round and listen to me tale: the terrifying tale of that infamous sea scoundrel Captain Gore. For fifty years, he terrorized the open seas. No friendly pirate was he. There be no funny cartoon stories about his kind. Take me word for it, mateys. You wouldn't want to cross swords with Gore or his cutthroat crew, the captain he-self being the most merciless pirate to ever pillage a village.

"Some say he weren't even human. That he were kin to a race of sea demons, which is why his left hand weren't no left hand at'all. It were a pincer. A giant claw, like that of a crab—which he used to snip off the heads of his enemies. And Captain Gore had a lot of enemies, he did.

"Men, women, children. Boys and girls alike. Anyone who refused to give up their loot, be it food or be it gold. But even a pirate be no match for one mother. That'd be Mother

Nature herself. For it were during a terrible storm when the *Bloodmere* ran aground in this very cove."

The lighthouse keeper pointed over the guardrail, to the waves crashing against the cliffs.

"They say he buried his booty along this coastline." Some of the students laughed and the lighthouse keeper had to explain: "Not *that* kind of booty. 'Booty' be another word for treasure. A treasure that's still out there, for not a single doubloon's been recovered. Landlubbers are still looking. Digging up and down the coastline. And some of 'em lost their lives looking. That be the curse, ya see. The curse of Captain Gore, for any foolish mortals lookin' to loot his loot. Dead men tell no tales." **Oh, I beg to differ.** "And the price you pay . . . off with yer heads!"

The old man swung his left arm around, revealing a pincer instead of a hand!

The students screamed and backed away as a unit. The lighthouse keeper laughed and he laughed, and it wasn't long before the students laughed with him. The pincer was a rubber prop available in the gift shop. The class applauded, all except one kid. That obnoxious one in the back. His name was Chris. "Is that it?" he blurted. "Can we finally climb up to the top?"

The lighthouse keeper shaded his eyes so he could make out who it was. He saw the boy. The obnoxious one wearing a shirt with an obnoxious slogan (not suitable for printing). "No," the lighthouse keeper responded. "That weren't it. There be more, if you'd care to hear it?"

The class said yes. Chris simply shrugged.

The old man looked serious—or as serious as you could look wearing a rubber pincer. "On certain nights, when the storm's just right, you can still see the *Bloodmere* adrift in these misty waters, glowing like a firefly. A ghost ship, she is. And if you keep on watching, you'll see where Captain Gore buried his gold."

The students sat in silence, enthralled. That is, until Chris blew a raspberry and the entire group laughed. Then he went further, as the obnoxious ones often do. "Have *you* seen it?" he asked the old man.

"Aye, lad. For certain, I have. When the storms be just as they were, the *Bloodmere* returns. In all her gory glory."

"Then how come you didn't take their booty? I mean, you work in a lighthouse—for what? Minimum wage? You might as well be flipping burgers." This incited more giggling, the students no longer laughing *with* the lighthouse keeper but *at* him.

The old man kept his eyes focused on Chris. "'Cause I remember the code, laddie, as should you. Dead men tell no tales."

Just then, Ms. Fisher stepped to the front of the class to do damage control. She also had some disappointing news to report. The remainder of the lighthouse tour had been canceled. A storm was coming in from the south, and the last ferry would be leaving for the mainland in twenty minutes. That gave them ten minutes in the gift shop.

In the meantime, Chris convinced his less obnoxious pals, Jaycie and Niles, to ditch the gift shop so they could keep watch while he climbed to the top of the lighthouse. That doesn't sound like a big deal, since lighthouses have spiral staircases—built specifically for climbing—that lead to observation decks. Except on that day, an electrical storm, the likes of which could bring a cadaver to life *(see previous tale)*, was bearing down on the region, meaning a climb to the top was strictly prohibited.

Except for the obnoxious ones. They had no rules. They'd climb anything.

Chris knew he had about ten minutes before Ms. Fisher would start counting heads. Just enough time to climb. To post a shot from the top deck—the pirate's hat—simply to prove he had done it. That was his thing: posting pictures of things he'd done that no one else would do. Hey, it was good to be known for something, right? *Right?*

As soon as the lighthouse keeper went on his break, Jaycie and Niles stood guard as Chris ducked under a chain and began his ascent. The first two flights felt like nothing. He was a healthy young "laddie," after all. But by level three, he was already feeling fatigued. He stopped for a break, inside the pirate's booty. (This time, we don't mean treasure.) All of a sudden, the tower vibrated. There was a great boom, like the sound of cannon fire. Had the *Bloodmere* returned to destroy the island? Jaycie hollered up the tower. "Yo, Chris, did you feel that thunder? You better come down!"

"Not on your life!" *Or . . . dare I say it? Never mind.*

Now more determined than before, Chris went straight to the top deck, the brim of the pirate's hat. Black clouds had blotted out a previously perfect sky. Now they were unleashing their burden, a storm of supernatural proportions.

Below, Jaycie and Niles ran for cover. The gift shop, their best option, was in range.

Greeted by thunder and lightning and pelted by rain, Chris ventured onto the outer deck. Waves were cascading against the

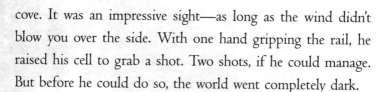

cove. It was an impressive sight—as long as the wind didn't blow you over the side. With one hand gripping the rail, he raised his cell to grab a shot. Two shots, if he could manage. But before he could do so, the world went completely dark.

Black storm clouds enveloped the lighthouse. Chris could no longer see, let alone take a picture. At the same time, he felt his feet rising from the deck. The wind had taken hold of his legs, and before he knew what was happening, Chris was flying. He let go of his cell so he could hold on to the rail with both hands. The loss of a phone didn't compare with what else he was about to lose: his life! Chris cried out for help, but the storm—a storm more obnoxious than even he was—swallowed his voice. *Don't let go,* he kept repeating in his head. *You'll die if you let go!*

But the rain had done a number on his grip, pelting away at his fingers. Chris felt himself slipping away. He was going to fall. This was the end. But the moment before Chris succumbed, he saw it.

A ship had emerged from the eye of the storm, like a glowing teardrop in the abyss. It was the *Bloodmere*, rising and dipping along the wavy coastline. It had three masts: the one in the middle flew a Jolly Roger, the skull and crossbones flag of a pirate vessel.

Chris studied the ship with a gamer's intensity, the storm no more than a minor inconvenience now. Less than a hundred yards away, a vision out of some glorious pirate past had unfolded. He watched as a specter disembarked from the gangplank of the phantom vessel. A stout man with a black beard, a white do-rag with red speckles, a white shirt, black pants—oh, and a pincer for a hand. A real one, not available at the gift shop. It had a pinkish hue and double rows of sharp white teeth on the insides of the claw. A pair of shipmates went ashore with Gore. They were carrying a weathered chest, and Chris instantly knew what it was. He was obnoxious, true, but he was also a good listener. It was Captain Gore's booty!

On orders from their captain, the pirates lugged the chest into the fourth cave in the cliff. There were hundreds of caves, by the way; if you looked it up on an antique map, Displeasure Island resembled a giant piece of Swiss cheese.

Chris witnessed the whole thing. And a moment later, he saw the pirates emerge from the cave without the chest. If his eyes hadn't deceived him, he'd seen where they had hidden their treasure! But the last thing he saw before he fell was a scene of unmitigated horror. Captain Gore had ordered the pirates to their knees. And immediately thereafter, without hesitation, he swiftly snipped off their heads with his pincer. The headless pirates remained momentarily upright. Could their disembodied heads still see what was happening from the sand? *Chris saw.* He saw what the heads could not. He saw Captain Gore, staring back at him from across time.

Remembering gravity, the headless pirates slumped forward at precisely the same moment. And before Chris even screamed—and he did, you know—the black cloud banished the vision back into the past. But it was too late for Chris. He had seen it. A sick sensation entered his body, and forgetting where he was, he opened his hands and dropped from the observation deck; the wind caught him and spun him around like a doomed kite before letting him go.

When Chris opened his eyes, the faces of students, teachers, and chaperones were staring down at him. He had been moved on a blanket into the gift shop. A student saw him wiggle his finger, and burst out screaming: "He's alive! Alive!" It was Juleen from science; she really had to come up with a new opening line.

Ms. Fisher rubbed his hand. "You okay, Chris? Did you break anything?"

He tried sitting up, but his body felt like one big bruise.

Yet remarkably, he was in one piece. The wind had buffered his fall. "I'm okay. I must have passed out."

"You don't look okay," said Jaycie, rubbing his other hand.

Niles added, "You look like you just saw a ghost."

Chris looked his way. "What made you say that?"

Then he heard the laughter. Not *with* him—*at* him. The sea of students parted, clearing a path for the old lighthouse keeper. "I found this on the beach. Afraid the pictures ya took won't do ya much good now." He was holding Chris's waterlogged cell phone. Seeing the fear in Chris's eyes, he laughed some more. "Whatever you seen's just a memory. Just a memory."

A terrifying memory, thought Chris. One that would rear its decapitated head again and again and again.

Chapter Seven

A PIRATE'S DEATH . . . (PART 2)

It wasn't until they were back on the mainland, a few days later, that Chris told Jaycie and Niles about his sensational find. "I know where it's hidden."

They were in Chris's bedroom, playing a computer game called *Pirate's Blood*. Niles never even looked away from the screen. "Where what's hidden?"

"Captain Gore's booty."

Jaycie placed her hand on Chris's forehead. "Take two aspirin and call me in the morning."

"I saw the whole thing!" he snapped.

"Before or after you fell?" Jaycie asked.

He shot her the most irritated look he could muster. "Before, moron-ski! I saw a pirate ship crash into a sandbar, just like the old geezer said it happened. And then I saw Captain Gore and a couple of his pirate pals carrying a treasure chest into a cave. And after that . . . Captain Gore cut off their heads." He did a *snip-snip* gesture with two fingers.

Niles looked up from the game. "Why would he do that to his pals?"

Chris shrugged. "I dunno. I guess to prevent them from saying where he hid his booty."

Niles chuckled. *That* word. It still got to him. "Makes sense, I guess."

"Excuse me?" Jaycie smacked his arm. "What he just said—that makes sense to you? That Chris saw something that happened like two hundred years ago?"

Niles, who was mostly known for talking before thinking, promptly retracted his thought. "Sorry, Chris. She makes more sense."

As usual, Chris had lost all patience with his pals. Niles with his gap-toothed grin and Jaycie with her mile-long chin—they were far from perfect. *Far from him.* Chris

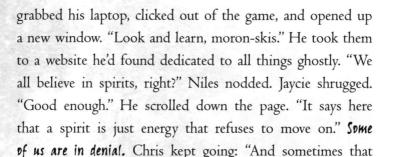

grabbed his laptop, clicked out of the game, and opened up a new window. "Look and learn, moron-skis." He took them to a website he'd found dedicated to all things ghostly. "We all believe in spirits, right?" Niles nodded. Jaycie shrugged. "Good enough." He scrolled down the page. "It says here that a spirit is just energy that refuses to move on." *Some of us are in denial.* Chris kept going: "And sometimes that energy keeps replaying itself, like a song or a scene from a movie. It's called"—he scrolled farther down until he found the word—"retrocognition."

"What movie is that?" questioned Niles. "I never heard of it."

"Not the movie, moron-ski, the word! Instead of seeing the spirit of a person, you see the spirit of an event. Usually one that's linked to a tragedy."

"Like a doomed pirate ship," added Jaycie.

"Uh-huh."

Another moment passed. "How come you got to see it?" Niles asked. Chris and Jaycie both looked his way simultaneously. For Niles, that was a reasonably thoughtful question. And Chris had spent the past few days thinking about the answer.

"As far as I can figure, it has to do with the storm. The conditions were just right. Maybe the vision was stuck in the clouds. Or the thunder woke it up."

Jaycie shook her head. "That sounds pretty out there to me. Even from you, matey."

Chris pointed to the door. "There's the hatchway, lassie." He turned to Niles. "What about you? Are you still with me on this?"

"With you where? I don't even know what you're talking about!"

"Take a wild guess. I'm talking about everything you ever wanted! New kicks. New digs. A trip around the world. You name it!"

Now even Jaycie was starting to come around. As crazy as it sounded, there was always that slim chance—one in a million doubloons—that what Chris claimed he had seen had actually happened. She'd put up with enough of his nonsense schemes in the past. Why should she miss out on the one that might pay off? "I didn't say I wasn't in . . . Captain. What exactly are you proposing?"

"The treasure. Captain Gore's booty. It's worth millions." He *snip-snip*ped with his imaginary pincers, pretending to cut off Jaycie's nose and Niles's ear. "Arrrrrr! I be Captain Gore, and you, mateys, arrrrrrre me helpers. Raise your left pincers and swear allegiance or it's off with yer heads!"

Jaycie and Niles raised their hands, making peace-sign pincers and, between giggles, pledged allegiance to the pirates' flag. "Arrrrrrrr!"

"The last ferry departs at six, mateys," said Chris, and he clicked on the schedule.

Niles didn't like the sound of it. "You mean . . . tonight?"

"I saw it on a news site. Displeasure Island is vacant because of the storm. It's practically a ghost town right now." *Try literally. . . .* "There're just some workers and that old geezer in the lighthouse. That means fewer witnesses to worry about."

Jaycie exchanged looks with Niles. Admittedly, it sounded exciting, even adventurous, the perfect Friday-night excursion. Better than miniature golf. But talking about it was a lot saner than actually doing it. And there was something Jaycie hadn't thought of. Something the usually less thoughtful Niles had figured out all by himself. "If you're Captain Gore, then that makes us your pals."

"Aye!"

"You said Captain Gore murdered his pals. You said he chopped off their heads."

"Aye!" Chris made pincer fingers. "So I did, mateys." *Snip-snip.*

The trio of friends watched from the top deck of the ferry as Displeasure Island came into range. The floating dock appeared first, through a thinning fog.

Chris pointed. "Land ho! Shiver me timbers! Me treasure awaits!"

Jaycie wasn't sure she liked the "me" part, but she said nothing. As usual.

As for Niles, he was privately wondering why he and Jaycie had ever become friends with Chris in the first place, an idea that officially tipped the scales and made him a thoughtful thinker. Before hooking up with Chris, he and Jaycie had never gotten into any real trouble. In fact, Niles had been something of a teacher's pet, which was pretty rare for a boy with middling grades.

But after he met Chris, everything changed.

Chris, you see, had a certain talent: a knack for talking people into doing things they wouldn't normally do. Niles was his most gullible target, but he worked the same obnoxious magic on Jaycie, as well.

As the ferry glided into the first stall, the threesome saw the lighthouse, the 168-foot-tall pirate welcoming them ashore. *Or was it Captain Gore, warning them to leave?*

"Bring the bag!" ordered Chris, referencing an equipment bag filled with gardening tools. Apparently, captains didn't do bags. "See you on the beach, mateys." And he ran down the ferry stairs, leaving Jaycie and Niles to deal with all the grunt work.

With Chris leading the charge, Jaycie and Niles lugged the equipment across the sandy coastline, getting soaked by cascading waves. Even the gulls seemed to get a laugh out of it. "How much further?" Jaycie asked, doing her best *I'm with the program* voice.

"Why? You got something better to do?" asked their obnoxious leader.

"Nope."

"Then no more comments from the peanut gallery." Chris kept moving, undeterred. "Our destination's directly ahead!"

Jaycie could no longer hide her anger, her mile-long chin

turning red. Niles just looked confused, his thoughts as empty as the enormous gap in his teeth. "I don't see a cave, I see a mountain," Jaycie said.

"I'm with her," added Niles.

Chris rolled his eyes before pointing. "It's behind it, moron-skis—uh, mateys. It's directly behind it!" The "it" he'd been referencing was a massive stone obstruction, covered in moss and green slime and embedded with shells. The sea had decorated it over time.

Jaycie dropped her half of the bag, and Niles, unable to manage the rest, dropped his half, too. "It doesn't look like a treasure chest," he said.

Jaycie gave a snort. She was annoyed, feeling duped by Chris for the umpteenth time. "I hope you're not serious. We'd need a keg of dynamite to blast through that thing." She slapped the wall. "It's as solid as, like, a rock or something."

Chris was grinning; he couldn't help it. "Who needs dynamite?" He unzipped the bag, revealing two brand-new shovels taken from his stepfather's toolshed. "We're not going through it, we're going under it." He stepped over by the wall and made an X in the sand below it, showing them precisely where to dig. "Two hundred years ago, there was an entrance.

It's under the sand now. That's why no one could find it."

He removed both shovels and handed one to Niles, the other to Jaycie. "I'll keep watch," he said, "just in case that creepy old geezer comes by."

Reluctantly, Jaycie accepted a shovel. "And why, may I ask, do we get to do all the digging?"

"Because *I'm* the captain!" replied Chris. And seconds later, Jaycie and Niles were digging. Of course, it wasn't the most intelligent answer. But truth be told, the answer worked back in pirate days, so why not now? Chris had always been their captain. Not by hire, or election, or even mutiny. He was their captain because they allowed it.

It took a little over two hours for Jaycie and Niles to find the entrance under the sand. That's in real time. **For you, foolish reader, it only took a sentence.** They were exhausted and covered in so much sand it was literally coming out of their ears.

It was time for Chris to take over. He directed his stepfather's flashlight—the one he had been warned not to touch—into the hole. He could make out a crawl space under the sand. An entrance, just like he'd said there would be. "See! What'd I tell ya? You guys keep watch. I'm going in!"

This time there were no objections. If Chris was crazy enough to crawl into a pitch-black hole, he had earned his captain stripes.

"Wish me luck, mateys." Chris couldn't see what lay ahead. The flashlight didn't reveal much. But the briny scent of the sea was overwhelming. He thought he might lose his lunch. Four slices of pizza, Niles's treat. Fortunately, visions of a buried treasure kept his stomach in line.

Jaycie and Niles watched his legs disappear into the chasm beneath the sand. The last they saw of Chris were the soles of his cheap sneakers, and Jaycie was thinking that when it came to moron-ski moments, this one took the cake. She looked at Niles and said something similar out loud. "This is the dumbest thing he's ever done."

Before Niles returned a comment, a black cloud passed over the cove, blotting out the entire sky. It was a cloud that looked hauntingly familiar.

Chris was an obnoxious young man; it's been well established. He played by his own rules, and sometimes others paid the price. But did he deserve what happened next? *I'd say yes, but you know me. I prefer it when things get messy.*

He was about ten feet into the narrow stone shaft, worming his way through a layer of thick, slimy mud. It was like crawling through peanut butter—and with the various rocks, shells, and crab carcasses mixed in, we're talking chunky style.

Creeping forward, Chris wondered how long the stone tube went on for. The air was thick, putting a strain on his lungs. He took intermittent breaths. Seawater was dripping in through the fissures above his head. He could taste the salt; it made him spit. His arms were too constricted even to wipe his mouth. He knew that if he got stuck—and the tide came in—a slow death would be a certainty. But he also knew that the trek would be worth it. To be the richest kid in his two-bit town, Chris would crawl into a pirate's cave.

A few more feet and breathing became easier. Chris felt the walls widening as the tunnel expanded into a cave. Still on his belly, he panned the flashlight. He had made it inside a small stone recess, no more than thirty feet from wall to wall.

"Chris! You alive down there?" It was either Jaycie or Niles. He didn't know which. And he no longer cared. The richest kid in town didn't need friends—or anyone else, for that matter. In fact, now that he'd made it safely inside, he regretted bringing them along in the first place. He was the one who had seen the ghost ship. He knew where the booty was. Why should he share it with anyone?

"Chris, the storm's coming!" That was Jaycie. "We have to get out of here!"

"Do what ya gotta do!" responded Chris. And Jaycie immediately recognized his dismissive voice. Chris didn't care what happened to his pals as long as he got what he had come for.

"Did you find anything?" asked Niles.

There was a long pause before Chris responded. "No, there's nothing here! Go inside! This was a wasted trip! Sorry, mateys!"

And right away, Jaycie identified that voice, too. It was Chris's lying voice.

He'd found something, all right. He had spotted it a second earlier with his stepfather's flashlight: a wooden chest was sticking out of the muddy ground. It was the same one he had seen in the ghostly vision. And he had already decided to keep every last doubloon for himself. After all, he'd found it. Maybe that wasn't the pirates' code, but it was Chris's. *Finders keepers, losers weepers.*

And the mere thought brought him to his feet. He

wouldn't crawl to the chest; he would walk there. The rich didn't do things on their knees. The rich brought others *to* their knees.

He took a first step and went sliding, almost cracking open his head on the wall. But that didn't slow him down. Chris could see the future; it was even clearer than the ghostly past. Untold riches were less than twenty feet away. Delicious thoughts swirled through his head. He would buy the middle school and have it shut down. Better yet, he'd have it torn down. Yes, there be a cold heart beating in his obnoxious chest. **A pirate's heart . . . and soon its ghost. Arrrrrr!**

Meanwhile, Jaycie and Niles had climbed to the top of a sandbar, still looking for cover, when they heard a voice cry out. "Ahoy! Ahoy!" It was the lighthouse keeper, waving frantically from the observation deck. "This way, lad and lassie! Hurry!"

They ran to the lighthouse with their jackets over their heads, and by the time they got there, the old man was down at the bottom, handing them fresh Displeasure Island towels (available at the gift shop). Jaycie and Niles were soaked and shivering. They looked pretty pathetic, but that didn't stop the old man from lacing into them. "What were you two thinking? Or is it that you weren't thinking at'all?"

At first they didn't say. If they did, Chris would likely eviscerate them. **Every boy needs a hobby.** Thinking fast, Jaycie faked an excuse. "Niles here lost his wallet during the class trip and we came back on our own to find it."

Thinking less than fast, Niles said, "I don't own a wallet."

"That's because you lost it, moron-ski!"

The lighthouse keeper played along. "I keep the lost-and-found box up in the pirate's head. Follow me." He pointed to the top of the lighthouse. "Free tour."

Jaycie and Niles didn't want a free tour—not on that night. But they were in pretty deep, which came with the territory. It was just how it was, being friends with Chris.

"Watch where you step," the old man cautioned. "The stairs can be a mite slippery."

Jaycie exchanged weary looks with Niles. "Up we go, I guess." And up the spiral staircase they went as thunder cracked and lightning bolted across the night sky. They were feeling like they didn't have a choice when, in fact, they did. When your insides tell you not to do something, don't do it. But Jaycie and Niles shared the same weakness; it was a flaw that people like Chris preyed on. They simply didn't have the guts to say no.

The next round of thunder shook the entire structure, and Niles lost it. "Did you feel that? We're going to die!"

"Of course I felt it!" Jaycie replied.

"The structure is perfectly sound," said the lighthouse keeper, his voice calm and reassuring. "It was here before you both were born, it was, and it will be here after you're both six feet under." Okay, maybe *reassuring* wasn't the right word. Jaycie looked at Niles and one of them gulped. (It was Niles.)

They continued to climb, making it all the way to the pirate's head without incident. "You have arrived," said the old man. "The brains of the operation, I like to call this." It was the level where he'd spent most of his life. He invited Jaycie and Niles to look through the pirate's eyes . . . um . . . windows. "It feels like you're on top of the world."

They each took an eye . . . um . . . window.

The view was unlike anything they'd ever imagined. The ocean they sometimes swam in was a giant void, like outer space here on earth, stretching endlessly, concealing infinite secrets beyond its foam and crashing whitecaps. Jaycie and Niles had never felt so insignificant. So small.

Niles had to ask: "You stay up here by yourself all day?"

"Aye."

"I don't get it. What's there to do?"

The old man spoke with a pride as grand as the sea. "I watch," he said. "I can see the world from here. The sun rising. The crabs migrating. Life, death. I see it all."

"What about Captain Gore?" asked Jaycie. "Did you ever see the *Bloodmere*? I mean, for real?"

The lighthouse keeper considered the question. And they could see him considering his response. But none was forthcoming. Instead, he turned his back to them and retreated to the opposite side of the deck. "I'd better fetch the lost-and-found box so you can be on your way."

Jaycie turned to Niles. Hard rain was pounding the windows—the eyes of the pirate. "Do you think we should tell him about Chris? Before the storm gets worse?"

Niles didn't hear her. He was straining to see something through the left eye. Something bigger than their obnoxious pal. There was a ship out there—a glowing vessel entering the universe from the black cloud. "Jaycie . . ."

"What?"

Niles was speechless. He needed Jaycie to see it for herself. He pointed to the other window. Jaycie pressed her face to the glass and stared out over the sea.

"Do you see what I see?" Niles was hoping she'd say yes.

Jaycie didn't answer, at least not with words. Her mouth had opened involuntarily, and that was confirmation enough. Yes, she saw it, too. They both did. Just like the old man knew they would.

The perfect storm had facilitated its return. A pirate ship—glowing, pulsating, luminescent green—was rising and falling with the waves. It was the *Bloodmere*, replaying a scene, as it had many times since it had sunk. What had Chris called it? Jaycie remembered and said the word out loud. "Retrocognition."

They watched with shock, with awe, as the ghost of the notorious Captain Gore came ashore, with his pirate pals carrying a treasure chest. The apparitions moved along the sand and entered one of the many caves in the Swiss cheese wall, visible from the past. It was the fourth entrance, the same cave Chris was in now!

"The curse! They'll find him! They'll find Chris and they'll chop off his head!" shouted Niles.

Jaycie agreed. "We have to try to warn him!"

Just then, a shadow came to a stop behind them. Jaycie sensed it first. She gave Niles a swat and together they turned.

The lighthouse keeper was behind them, holding a

cardboard box with LOST & FOUND printed on the side. "Sorry, no wallets," said the old man. Jaycie and Niles tried to act surprised, but explaining away a white lie was the least of their worries.

The old man knew. He could see it in their eyes: a fear he understood well. "You seen it, then, aye?"

Jaycie nodded. "Yes, sir."

And Niles added, "Our friend's in a cave. The same one where they put their treasure!"

"What should we do?" asked Jaycie.

The lighthouse keeper had an answer—one they should have seen coming; his smirk should have given it away. "You die," he said. "Dead boys and girls tell no tales."

An explosion of thunder rocked the lighthouse, the tremor taking out the lights. It was pitch black inside. Jaycie and Niles blindly felt their way to each other, seeing nothing until a bolt of lightning flickered in through the pirate's eyes. And in that moment, they saw the old man's true self. That is, the true self he had corroded into. The lighthouse keeper was half skeleton, half rotted flesh; he wore tattered pirate clothes that hung from his shoulders like shredded rags.

Jaycie and Niles were too petrified to move. The lighthouse keeper raised his left arm, and they saw a pincer instead of a hand, this one not made of rubber. They didn't even get the chance to scream. . . .

Snip-snip!

From the outside, it looked like the eyes of the 168-foot-tall pirate were shedding tears of blood.

Inside the cave, Chris had already extracted the chest from the mud, all the while singing: "Yo-ho, yo-ho, a pirate's death for me . . ." He broke open the lock with the butt of his stepfather's flashlight and was about to open the chest when a luminescent glow overtook the cave. He released the lid to see what he assumed would be a scene from the distant past. In fact, he was looking forward to it. Like a favorite movie moment. This would be the scene that made him rich.

A pirate apparition entered the cave, just as Chris had anticipated. He knew it was Captain Gore from his pincer, now dripping with blood. But Chris's terror reached a petrifying peak when he saw the captain's features. The face was that of the old lighthouse keeper. He and Captain Gore were one and the same.

But that wasn't all he saw. As the scene continued to unfold . . .

Two more specters entered the cave: Gore's pirate helpers,

carrying the treasure chest. The captain ordered it buried, and the pirates began to dig. They dug without protest. Up close, Chris could see their faces, too. But it couldn't be. How?

HOW?

The pirates were Jaycie and Niles, now a part of the past, in a scene that would repeat itself, over and over and over. . . .

That's retrocognition for you.

Chris got up into their faces. "Wait! Don't listen to him! Say no! Don't do it! Just say no!"

Chris waved his arms, but it was no use. They couldn't hear him. Not that it would have mattered. Jaycie and Niles never said no.

Captain Gore slowly turned toward Chris, and as the old ghost pirate raised his pincer, the luminescent glow that surrounded the pirates burned brighter than ever before—so bright, in fact, that Chis had to avert his eyes. A moment later, the images dissolved into nothingness. The scene had played out. The figures were gone; the storm had moved on, taking the past with it. Chris spun around, searching for the pirates, but there was nothing there. He was alone in the cave once more, terrified beyond all reason, his body shaking. He stood there for hours, not moving, barely breathing.

Until the dawn came. He heard the calming sounds of the morning sea. The surf was settling; the gulls had returned.

Chris had stood there all night. Now, with the arrival of dawn, the terror had left the cave. As if he had woken up from a nightmare, Chris was slowly feeling like his old obnoxious self again. He went back to the chest to finish what he had started. The moment had come. His moment. He clutched the lid and thought, *This is the last time I won't be the richest kid in town.* Then he opened it to gloat over his treasure.

He saw a treasure, all right.

Resting in a mound of gold doubloons was a pair of human skulls staring back at him. And even without their skins, Chris recognized whom they had once belonged to by the mile-long chin on one and the gap-toothed grin on the other.

He dropped the lid, no longer interested in gold, and spun around to leave. The small shaft of light from the entrance abruptly disappeared. To his horror, the cave had once again been sealed—no way in, no way out. *Or if you prefer: no windows and no doors.*

"Heeeeeelp!" he cried, because they all try that one. "Somebody help me!" He tried that one, too. He tried every variation of *help* you could think of until his vocal cords gave out. And then he searched for an exit in every conceivable crevice until his stepfather's flashlight gave out.

It was the very last time Chris was ever seen . . . but not the last time he was heard. He now lives in the tales told by the old lighthouse keeper. The latest iteration involves an obnoxious kid who dared defy the pirate code of Captain Gore and got all the treasure that was coming to him.

Snip-snip!

Chapter Eight

GHOST RELATIONS

———— ❦ ————

"**S**nip-snip!" said Prudence Pock, and she closed the book with a snap. Immediately following the tale, Dr. Ackerman excused himself from room 4, saying he had an errand to run. Prudence Pock had on that dubious grin she wore so well. "Don't be long, Doctor. There's still one more tale to tell."

The reflected light of the orderly's candelabrum drew near as the doctor exited room 4. "Will you be breaking for a meal?"

Dr. Ackerman spun around, startled, his exhaled breath

extinguishing the candles. Or had it? A second later, the flames arose on their own. Dr. Ackerman found his composure. "A meal? No. I'm taking a little trip to a cemetery."

"Ah, a most pleasant diversion. Have we an appointment with a departed soul?"

The doctor looked at him oddly. "Nothing of the sort, Coats. It's to lay to rest a patient's claim, that a mansion resides beyond the graveyard. If it does, I'm going to find it."

"So you have accepted the possibility of its existence? Or is it *impossibility*? I never can get that right." The orderly slipped his gloved hand into his inside pocket and checked the time on an antique pocket watch. "You can just make it before sundown." Dr. Ackerman headed up the corridor, almost past the security doors, when the orderly called out, "Oh, and, sir . . ."

"What is it now, Coats?"

The orderly smiled. "Hurry baaa-aack."

The details of Dr. Ackerman's errand involved a trip to Route 13. Driving up the single-lane path, Dr. Ackerman noticed a slew of commemorative wreaths, dwarfed by blackened trees concealing who knew what. There were bats dangling from

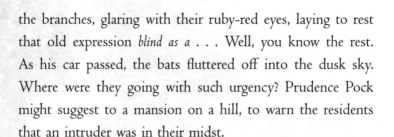

the branches, glaring with their ruby-red eyes, laying to rest that old expression *blind as a . . .* Well, you know the rest. As his car passed, the bats fluttered off into the dusk sky. Where were they going with such urgency? Prudence Pock might suggest to a mansion on a hill, to warn the residents that an intruder was in their midst.

Yet if such a place existed, why didn't it show up on Dr. Ackerman's GPS? All he could see was the glowing outline of a capacious graveyard at the end of Route 13. **Dead ahead, as we say in the trade.** Maybe the answers *lay* in there.

A cemetery is sometimes referred to as a *necropolis*. That is, a city of the dead. And the Eternal Grace Cemetery more than lived up to the designation. It was a city populated by tombstones, a private district of the deceased. The grave markers appeared never-ending. Along with the tears, Dr. Ackerman surmised.

Death was final, was it not? That was what Dr. Ackerman believed. He had never been visited by an "expired" relative. There were no spirits; there was only sorrow. The only things at rest below those markers, Dr. Ackerman believed, were dust and decay. As for the inscriptions themselves, a name and a slogan were all the remains of a life that had been lived.

Lost in his thoughts, he didn't notice the ground fog swirling in by his feet. He'd been preoccupied, reading the epitaphs on a pair of grave markers.

Forgetting where he was, Dr. Ackerman laughed. He laughed because death suddenly seemed less serious. The amusing epitaphs made the inevitable less foreboding. At least, momentarily. He recalled his father's final words: "We all gotta go sometime. Why not go with a smile?" *His father hadn't noticed the speeding train. His smile arrived at the next station ten minutes ahead of schedule.*

And then the doctor heard someone saying those same words aloud. "We all gotta go sometime."

He spun around, half expecting to see his expired father. That was before he remembered where he was. There was a white-haired man, wearing a scarf and hat, with a trembling bloodhound at his side. The man lifted a lantern, adding yellowish hues to his complexion. He was the caretaker.

"What did you say just now?" Dr. Ackerman asked.

"I was just telling the gent over there we all gotta go sometime." The caretaker motioned toward a mourner in the next row who was sobbing over a grave.

"That's not for you to judge. We all grieve in our own ways."

The caretaker locked eyes with the doctor, his expression gravely serious. "The dead don't like it, sir. That sort of behavior, it prevents 'em from movin' on."

"There is no moving on for the dead." Dr. Ackerman was unwavering in his opinion.

"The ones who've been wronged, sir. Those who've been murdered and whatnot. They can't move on. Their kind's got unfinished business to attend to."

The remark greatly irritated Dr. Ackerman. "You are an authority, I take it? An expert on the murdered and whatnot?"

"No, not an expert. I'm just the caretaker." The caretaker tipped his cap and kept moving.

"Just a moment!" the doctor called out. "What can you tell me about a mansion on a hill? I've made several inquiries in town. No one cares to acknowledge it, which leads me to believe it doesn't exist. I even asked some hitchhikers on Route 13."

The caretaker shuddered. So did his dog. "You didn't give them a ride, did you?"

"Heavens, no! Unsavory types, the lot of them."

The caretaker nodded. "The type that follow you home." He continued on, only this time Dr. Ackerman followed.

"Were they from the mansion?" There was a hesitation in the caretaker's step. "You've seen it, haven't you?"

"I've seen many things . . . I ought not talk about."

The doctor removed a gold watch from his wrist. "This belonged to my father. He wasn't a very nice man but he had expensive things. Show me the mansion and it's yours."

The bloodhound starting barking, and it took a moment

for the caretaker to settle him down. Afterward, he said, "It's not mine to show. It's yours to see. When you're ready." And with that, the caretaker and his trusted canine companion ambled off, disappearing behind the headstones.

The sun had begun to set below the cemetery gates. The darkness was coming, but Dr. Ackerman couldn't leave yet. Was the mansion Prudence Pock spoke of more than just part of a madwoman's musings? If it existed, why couldn't he find it on a map? He could find no such dwelling. Nothing but unending tributes to the dead. Had they all been hallucinating? Had Route 13, the graveyard, or both produced some sort of mass hysteria?

The night was upon him now, and the usually discerning Dr. Ackerman found himself grateful to the moon. Of course, shadows of varying shapes and sizes came with it, but he'd worry about those later. For the moment, the emphasis was on getting back to Shepperton Sanitarium. Prudence Pock had one more tale to tell. *Her* tale. Perhaps the answers lay buried in her prose.

His walk became a trot, and soon Dr. Ackerman was running. The parking lot was in range; he could see its unusual sign: DEAD END—PREPARE TO EXIT TO THE LIVING

WORLD. But a specific grouping of gravestones slowed him down. As desperate as he was to leave, he had to stop and read the epitaphs:

SHELLEY'S BRAIN
WOULD TAKE HER FAR
IF IT WASN'T FOR THAT
SPEEDING CAR

AHOY THERE, CHRIS!
YOU'LL HAVE NO REST
BURIED WITH A
PIRATE'S CHEST

Dr. Ackerman felt like he could explode! *Mops please, janitors. Confound that woman! She made it all up! Those tales. She saw the graves and made it all up.* He would lace into her when he got back. If he got back. Because even Dr. Ackerman didn't expect to see the next tombstone:

The doctor made it back to the sanitarium in record time. If Officer Davis had still been on the job, there would have been a citation. He was back inside the dungeon corridor, having squeezed himself out of the elevator before the doors fully opened. The orderly had been waiting to greet him. "Good evening, Doctor. Is something wrong? You seem unusually distressed."

"I am! That's the perfect way to put it, Coats! I'm unusually distressed!"

"Perhaps a cup of warm milk or some tea would help soothe your frazzled nerves?" But Ackerman didn't even bother to acknowledge the orderly's suggestion. He headed directly to room 4, snapping his fingers, impatiently waiting for Coats to do his job. "The key, man! Open up! Before I kick it in!"

"Yes, sir. Right away, sir." The orderly turned the key.

The door creaked open and Dr. Ackerman entered the padded room. It was frightfully chilly in there. Colder than the graveyard. Looking around, Dr. Ackerman couldn't see her . . . at first.

"Prudence?"

The door slammed behind him. Dr. Ackerman heard the key turn and the lock fasten. He could see the orderly's eyes through the rectangular slot in the door. Coats slowly slid the panel on the slot shut, blocking out the light.

The doctor turned and found Prudence on her stool. She was smiling as if she'd always been there. "Welcome back, good doctor. You look as if you've seen a ghost. Or two or three or four."

"There are no ghosts!" **Ahem!** "What kind of a stunt are you trying to pull? Is Coats in on this, too? Do you have the whole asylum in on your little game?"

"Game, Doctor? You must have me confused with your other patients."

Dr. Ackerman took a long breath, trying to restore a semblance of professionalism. He ran his fingers through his hair, threw back his shoulders to straighten his posture, then stepped toward Prudence. "I didn't mean to shout. I've just returned from the cemetery. I saw headstones bearing the names of your protagonists. You, my dear, are an imposter. Prudence Pock is dead."

Her grin expanded. "So she is," she gleefully confirmed. "Do you, perchance, remember how I died? Think back for me, Doctor, to the role *you* played in this final tale. A tale that binds us together, forever and ever." Dr. Ackerman knew he didn't have to respond. He was going to hear it either way. *Just like you, foolish reader.* "Let me remind you, Dr. Ackerman."

Dr. Ackerman looked for the door, hoping to once again see the orderly's eyes in the rectangular slot.

But the door was no longer there.

"Sit," said Prudence, and the second stool slid in behind Dr. Ackerman. He surrendered to her request. Prudence was holding volume four. "It's all here, Doctor. In this final tale from the Haunted Mansion." She opened the book, the pages turning on their own before stopping on the last story. Prudence Pock handed the book to Dr. Ackerman. For the final tale, she insisted he do the honors by reading it aloud.

Interlude

Pay attention!
When hinges creak in doorless chambers
and strange and frightening sounds
echo through the halls—that is
the time when ghosts are present,
practicing their terror with ghoulish delight.

All is not as it seems,
for our final tale is but a dream
within a dream.

Chapter Nine

WRITER'S BLOCK

It's almost over, Prudence Pock heard the voice inside her head say. The first visible signs of arthritis had crept in.

She was halfway through a signing event at Ye Olde Book Shoppe. A greatest hits package, as she cynically referred to it. Old wares in a new wrapping. Prudence Pock hadn't produced anything new in years, and the smattering of fans reflected it. She counted thirty-one in total.

Since the mysterious death of Rand Brisbane, Prudence Pock couldn't write a decent terror tale to save her skin. *Perhaps we can lend a hand. . . .* Maybe she had forgotten how to scare people. Yet there was little doubt that Prudence Pock remembered how to *get scared*.

A stranger had been staring at her from the far corner of the shop. Staring right through her, it felt like. He was a man in his forties. Tall, maybe six two, with a receding hairline. He was wearing a smart gray suit, the kind with a signature on the inside pocket, not available at the mall. *He must be a lawyer or a doctor,* she thought. *One of those highfalutin types everyone seems to admire but no one wants to see.* He had her book in his hand: *The Very Best of Prudence Pock.* Why hadn't he approached the table? Was he waiting for the "crowd" to depart?

In the midst of all that, Prudence received the mysterious invitation from an unseen girl with a clinking bracelet. **And as you're about to discover, that wasn't even the creepiest part of the evening.**

Prudence was on her way to her car when the stranger in the gray suit approached. Spotting him with her peripheral vision, she tried beating him to her car door. But he got there first. "Ms. Pock?"

"I'll scream," she said, trying to scare him off.

"Not as loud as I will. I'm your biggest fan!" He held up her book and took two steps back to prove that he wasn't a weirdo—which proved nothing. Weirdos are weirdos, no matter how far back they stand. "I'm sorry. I didn't mean to scare you. Imagine that. Someone like me scaring Prudence Pock."

She was scared; she had to admit it, if only to herself. "There's a schedule on my website. You can visit me at the next event." She reached for the door handle and the stranger reached for her hand. Prudence Pock heard the sound of her own heart beating, a cliché she'd used, oh, at least a dozen times. But being a cliché didn't make it untrue.

"Don't touch me," she said, and she looked back to see if the store security guard was still watching. He wasn't.

The stranger retracted his hand. "Once again, I apologize. I should have approached you in the store."

"Yes, that would have been the appropriate venue."

"I was nervous. I hope you understand. Being your biggest fan, I've played this out a million times in my head."

"Played what out?"

"This moment." He reached into the pocket of his fine gray suit, and Prudence felt the air leave her body. She had used that cliché, too, and it was only a matter of time before the one about her legs turning to jelly would come up. The stranger extended an item, his palms crisscrossed, like he was offering a communion wafer. "Will you accept this?" He presented her with an antique quill.

"It's lovely," she said, admiring the obsolete writing tool. "It looks very old."

"Nineteenth century," the stranger confirmed. "It'll help you write your next story." He grew breathless with excitement. "It belonged to the master."

"The . . . master? And to whom, exactly, are you referring?"

"Poe," he replied. "This is the actual writing instrument used by Edgar Allan Poe."

Prudence slid her glasses to the tip of her nose. She needed to get a better look at the quill. It looked authentically old; she'd give him that. But Poe? If the stranger could be believed, it belonged to the greatest terror writer the world had ever produced. It was too grand a gift to even consider taking.

"I can't accept such a gift."

"Why is that? I've accepted gifts from you. For years, your words have kept me company. And I know from your biography that you're a great admirer of Poe."

"Who isn't? He was the master. The rest of us are just his pupils."

He placed his hands over Prudence's, closing her arthritic fingers around the quill. "How does it feel?"

"It feels great," she said. "It feels like history." She momentarily forgot the acute swelling in her joints. "But I couldn't possibly accept it. Not without giving you something in return."

The stranger had an idea. "I know. How about this? I'll settle for an autograph." He extended his copy of her book.

In Prudence's mind, the trade was wildly uneven. Still, she found it impossible to resist. "Sold!" She took out a felt marker to sign. "Your name, sir?"

"Ackerman," replied the stranger. "Dr. Ackerman."

"Oh, a doctor of what?"

"The mind," he replied. "My area of expertise is madness."

It was like an alarm went off in her head. Prudence stopped signing and looked up, carefully studying his face. "Was it something I said?" he asked. He hoped he hadn't offended her.

He hadn't. It was just the opposite, in fact. Prudence was poring over his features because his was a face she knew. Dr. Ackerman was a semi-celebrity in his own right. "You're *the* Dr. Ackerman? I used your books in my research." She felt a little silly saying the next bit, but since she liked hearing it herself, why not give him the same courtesy? "I'm *your* biggest fan!" Now it would be Prudence prolonging the meeting. "I hope this isn't too forward, Doctor, but would you have coffee with me? I'd love to pick your brain."

The doctor was taken aback by her proposal. "As would I, as would I! But I have an even better idea. Join me in my home. I make *the* perfect cappuccino. Puts World o' Coffee's to shame." And then he put the cherry on top. "You simply must see my collection."

"What sort of collection?"

"My Poe collection, naturally. I own some of the rarest items in the world. Including the very desk he used to pen 'The Raven.'"

If Prudence Pock had any thoughts about turning down his invitation, they were already lost in the fog. A night like that would be too great to pass up. Cappuccinos with the exalted Dr. Ackerman. The world's rarest Poe collection. It sure beat falling asleep in front of a TV.

"Yes!" she responded, unable to mask her enthusiasm. The very thought made her feel like writing again.

Dr. Ackerman was telling the truth: his cappuccino was infinitely superior to World o' Coffee's. Prudence was sipping her third cup as she circled the doctor's great room. There was an old-fashioned fireplace and finely restored furnishings of considerable age, with golden light supplied by oil lamps. The doctor was a romantic, she decided. An old-fashioned gentleman at heart. She paused by a bookshelf to admire his set of Poe first editions. "Is this real? Or am I dreaming?"

He responded with a favored Poe line: "'All that we see or seem is but a dream within a dream.'" She looked away and saw the master staring back at her. There was a portrait of Poe hanging over the mantel, along with related artifacts: skulls, masks, stuffed ravens. But it was a brass shelf clock with a marble figure of the Red Death that betrayed the time. "Oh my, Doctor. We've talked for hours. I'm afraid I've overstayed my welcome." She placed her cup onto a tray and extended her hand. "Thank you for your hospitality. It was a most enjoyable evening." But the doctor did not shake her hand.

"I couldn't possibly let you leave, dear Prudence." He stood between her and the door. "Not before you've seen the collection."

"The collection?" She chuckled, slightly nervous. "I thought we were looking at it now."

"This?" The doctor laughed with mock disdain. "Nonsense. The real treasures are down below." He cupped his hand over the head of a ceramic raven and twisted the neck like a corkscrew. The fireplace wall parted, revealing a hidden passageway. "Are you up for the midnight tour?"

Prudence's shoulders tightened. Her intuition was telling her to say no. It was all too strange. Yet despite that, she had an insatiable curiosity, especially when it came to the strange. "I am wondering. What's down there?"

"The spirits of the dead," he replied. "Do you dare come see for yourself?" The doctor removed a lit candle from an iron sconce for light.

The dormant writer was alive inside her, dying to know what might be lurking within the dark passages below the handsome home. The seeds of a new tale, perhaps. The tale that would win her the top prize at Amicus Arcane's grand celebration the next evening.

"Okay, Doctor. A quick tour couldn't hurt. Fifteen minutes, then I'm on my way."

The doctor smiled. "That should be just enough time."

She shuffled over, barely lifting her feet. It almost looked like she was sleepwalking.

"This way, dear Prudence. Come meet the master." The doctor led Prudence into the entrance of the hidden passageway. On the opposite side of the fireplace, there was a narrow stone staircase that plunged into darkness. They made their descent. Once again, it was like a scene out of her fantastical fictions. The steps kept coming; Prudence lost count after twenty.

She noticed the air growing more repellent the lower they got. It was the fetid scent of death and decay; she recognized it from her research trips to crypts and morgues. "I'm afraid."

"You, Prudence Pock, afraid?" He laughed, and that time she could tell he was acting. The doctor didn't find her funny at all.

They reached level ground and Prudence felt something splash by her feet. She could see what looked like a pink shoelace squirming past. It was a rat's tail. "Mind your step, dear Prudence. It can get slippery down here." He shifted the candle back and forth, introducing a path. They were at the far end of a long stone tunnel. Dark liquids were oozing down the walls, as if the house itself was melting. The place was old and corrupt, she decided. Something terrible had happened down there. And something terrible would happen again. Prudence could tell just by standing in it.

"Where are we, Doctor?"

"In the catacombs below my home. The tour starts here. A Vincent Price narration would be most apropos, wouldn't you agree?"

Taking Prudence by the arm, he led her deeper into the tunnel. "Look about. Feast your eyes! Gorge yourself on its horrors. Its putrid decay!" Prudence noticed four chamber doors, two on each side: a medieval version of the dungeon below Shepperton Sanitarium. The doctor was eager to explain: "The estate once belonged to an unsavory gentleman. A baron from the old country whose cruelty was legendary—a cruelty worthy of Poe's tales. The story goes, he built this section for his wife and children. Seems they spent a lot of time down here. Years, in fact. Years."

He steadied the candle over the first door, allowing Prudence a look through its peephole. There was a collection of bones, a skeletal figure, hanging from shackles against the stone wall. The ribs were exposed, and Prudence saw a large black spider spinning a web where the heart used to be.

"That's a prop, I take it."

Dr. Ackerman smiled. "It's amazing what you can pick up at Parties 4 Smarties these days. Shall we continue?" He shifted the candle, leaving the first chamber in merciful darkness. Prudence felt her legs turn to jelly. She stumbled, and Dr. Ackerman had to catch her before she went down all the way. "Careful not to break your neck, dear. We're almost there. The highlight of the tour."

The doctor led her to a second chamber door. Through that peephole, Prudence saw a skeleton chained to a table, its torso sliced in half. "'The Pit and the Pendulum'!" exclaimed her tour guide, Dr. Ackerman. "I had Poe's ingenious device meticulously re-created, down to the most minute detail." With admiration he watched the pendulum swaying back and forth, and for the first time that evening, Prudence decided that her host was insane. **We here at the mansion refer to that as a slow learner. Or is it "slow burner"? I never can get that right.** She had to figure out a way to leave that dungeon. Sensing her trepidation, Dr. Ackerman grabbed her hand. "This way, dear Prudence. There's more! There's more!"

They stopped by a third chamber, and in horror beyond all reason, she saw a skeleton encased inside a glass coffin, frozen in the moment of death, the hands still pressing against the lid, fighting to free itself from . . .

"A premature burial!" exclaimed Dr. Ackerman, raising both arms into the air. Now he was boasting.

"Why are you doing this? I don't understand!"

"No, I don't imagine you would. I'll try to explain it in layman's terms. I was born with a dark impulse. My parents noticed it when I was a child, and did their best to discourage it. They sent me to the best doctors and, ultimately, to the best schools, where I became a leading expert on diseased and troubled minds. Minds such as my own. But that didn't squash the terrible urge.

"You, dear Prudence, did that for me, with your books, with your words. Those tales you wrote. They spoke to me. Your stories saved my life. And, in turn, the lives of others."

Prudence Pock nodded as she recalled: "I remember. One of your early books covered this disorder at length."

"Yes. The person I was diagnosing was me. Your words, Prudence Pock, gave me stability. I was the sanest person I knew."

"But since I stopped writing . . ."

He gestured toward the chambers. "Without your stories, I had only the master. But Poe only dreamed it. *I* made it a reality. I am the dream within the dream."

Prudence hadn't realized she had already stepped inside the fourth chamber. There was a desk with a lighted candle in a holder, along with a ream of paper and a quill. Despite the madman in front of her, curiosity got the better of her. "Is that it?" she asked. "The desk of Edgar Allan Poe?"

Without getting an answer, she heard hinges creaking behind her. Prudence turned to see the doctor pulling closed a barred door, trapping her inside the chamber. She took a breath, tried playing it cool. "Bravo, Doctor. Bravo! You've made your point. You scared Prudence Pock. Now I really must be going." She stepped over and gave the bars a tug. The door was locked, and Dr. Ackerman, peering in from the outer corridor, didn't seem to be joking.

Prudence took out her phone to call for help but couldn't get a signal. *Cell service in medieval dungeons is practically non-existent.* Prudence knew she was in serious trouble. "The skeletons," she began. "They're . . . real?"

"As real as you and I," replied Dr. Ackerman. "They were my patients. The ones who won't be missed."

"You won't get away with th—" The chamber became blurry and started to spin. Prudence teetered back. The enormity of the situation hit her like a ton of bricks. She was going to faint, and there was nothing she could do about it except crumple to the ground.

Prudence Pock opened her eyes. Had she been out for a minute? An hour? A century? Her surroundings were still a blur. Had she been dreaming? Was the entire night a dream within a dream? She could hear her tormentor, Dr. Ackerman, delivering some insane soliloquy, like a villain from one of her stories. One of those villains who didn't know they were mad. "Welcome back, dear Prudence. So good of you to join the party."

Prudence latched on to the desk, pulling herself to her feet. The world was just coming back into focus. She saw the figure of her tormentor beyond the chamber recess. A sense of unspeakable horror overwhelmed her.

The doctor was holding a trowel and standing next to a pile of bricks. He was erecting a wall beyond the bars! Like a moment out of Poe, he was walling Prudence Pock into the chamber. Walling her in alive.

She tried to scream and could hear the shrill sound bouncing around in her skull, yet nothing emerged from her mouth. All she could do was sit there and watch—watch as the doctor whistled while he worked.

Before long, Dr. Ackerman completed the first tier.

Prudence's eyes were tearing up, but her lids never went down and her pupils never wavered. All she could do was watch as Dr. Ackerman piled brick on top of mortar on top of brick on top of mortar.

Two hours passed. Then three. Then four.

Dr. Ackerman was close to the end now. Without a choice, Prudence had sat, paralyzed, for what felt like eternity, witnessing the creation of her tomb. Her final rest-ing place. **Not.**

Dr. Ackerman was down to the last brick. She could see his eyes peering in through the rectangular slot. "You may think me cruel. On the contrary: I've come to help you. As your biggest fan, I offer you this gift: the chance to eradi-cate your writer's block. On the desk before you—Poe's very desk—you will find a ream of paper and a quill, along with enough candlelight to last you till morning. Write your way out of your tomb, Prudence Pock. Pen your most terrifying tale and you'll be released. Otherwise"—he brought the final brick into position, ready to insert it—"you will be the first known author to die from writer's block."

Dr. Ackerman placed the last brick over the hole, wig-gling it into place. The chamber was completely sealed.

"Heeeelp!" she cried. "I'm trapped! Somebody help me! He's insane!" No one could hear her—not from the recesses of a facility built for swallowing screams.

Prudence had to calm down, to think rationally. She had two clear options. One: she could die and become the latest exhibit of Dr. Ackerman's tour of terror. Or two: she could give him what he wanted. She could sit behind Poe's desk and write her most terrifying tale of all.

The solution came in a flash. Writer's block, be gone! Prudence sat at the desk and picked up the quill. Her hand was trembling. It had been a long time, and the stakes had never been higher. Life and death, literally. Was she still capable of eliciting screams? She had no choice but to try.

By the shimmery glow of a solitary candle, Prudence began to write.

She wrote the tale of a madman who kept his patients locked away in a dungeon. Her arthritic hands couldn't record the details fast enough. Working from inside a tomb was an inspiration. The words flowed out of her. Indeed, it was her most terrifying tale of all. It was the tale of her own death.

Dr. Ackerman waited an entire month before venturing down into the secret catacombs below his home, his assumption being that Prudence Pock would have expired by then. Without food, without water, that was a given. But he was excited about the gift she'd left behind. The first new Prudence Pock story in years was his, all his.

With a sledgehammer slung over his shoulder, he made his way to the walled-up writer's room. *A fine piece of craftsmanship*, he thought, admiring his handiwork. *Not bad for a headshrinker.*

He struck the wall. *Thunk! Thunk! Thunk!* Over and over, until the bricks crumbled and a section collapsed, forming a hole large enough to pass through. Exchanging the sledgehammer for a high-powered flashlight, Dr. Ackerman ventured into the chamber. "Prudence, dear. Your deadline's up. What sort of a tale have you written for me?"

Dr. Ackerman shrieked when he saw her. He had expected to find a dead person—that went without saying—but he hadn't expected to find a happy one. The corpse of Prudence Pock was smiling. She was smiling as if a great big surprise was in store for Dr. Ackerman. **And it was.**

Dr. Ackerman peered across the room and saw her words, neatly stacked in the center of the desk. It was a handwritten manuscript, with its author, Prudence Pock, seated behind the desk, displaying her tickled grin. In her fossilized hand was Poe's quill, its tip still pressed to the paper.

The doctor stepped away, divorcing himself from the scene: the desk, the manuscript, the position of the quill. It was chillingly perfect. In an instant, he knew what to call his new exhibit. He'd name it *Writer's Block*.

With the fiendish task complete, Dr. Ackerman turned for the main corridor. There was still some cleaning up to do. But before climbing out, he heard a frenetic scratching from

behind. What was it? More rats? It sounded like scribbling—
like a pen moving speedily across paper! He turned to look,
leveling his light.

The beam moved across the chamber, stopping on Poe's
quill. It was moving on its own, writing the same phrase
across paper, across walls, across the face of Prudence Pock
herself. It was the title of her story:

*Memento Mori Memento Mori Memento Mori Memento Mori
Memento Mori Memento Mori Memento Mori Memento Mori Memento
Mori Memento Mori Memento Mori Memento Mori Memento Mori . . .*

Dr. Ackerman could feel the last vestiges of sanity escape
his skull. He had always been insane; perhaps he had been
born that way. But Prudence Pock's tales had helped him
control it. Now the madness was in control. He scrambled
to escape through the hole. But the last thing he saw was the
glowing arm of a ghost holding a trowel, bricking up the wall
from the outside. Dr. Ackerman was trapped inside a chamber . . . with no windows and no doors.

Trapped, as he had always been, within the endless corridors of his mind.

Chapter Ten

THE END IS NIGH

The eyes of the orderly were glaring in through the slot of room 4, a slot the size of a brick. With his hand trembling, Dr. Ackerman returned the book to Prudence Pock, the final tale complete. "Thank you, Doctor," she said. "You did a fine job reading. It even scared me, and I was there for it!"

He still had one question. "What about the mansion? Is it real?"

"Oh, yes. I attended the grand celebration I told you about. A carriage picked me up from Liberty Square the night *after* I died. Your actions provided me entry. It was a party that could only be attended by the dead."

"That's preposterous! Impossi—" The doctor stopped speaking. The book in his hands was opened to the title page, where an inscription read *To Dr. Ackerman, from your biggest fan—forever yours, Prudence Pock.* It was exactly as she had inscribed it in the Liberty Square parking lot, and it was dated four years earlier. Prudence Pock smiled. "Is all that we see or seem but a dream within a dream?"

The truth came flooding back to him, as it did every evening. "For four glorious years, Doctor, I've been visiting you inside this padded room, repeating the tale of your crimes. Watching the sanity drain from your eyes, night after night after night. The professional term is retrocognition."

Dr. Ackerman was no longer protesting. As it happened every night, he was starting to recall—to remember the ghastly details of the crime that had relegated him to his own asylum. And the more he remembered, the more he laughed. It was the laugh of the hopelessly insane, the ones they kept hidden in the dungeon like dirty little secrets.

Prudence rose from the stool and floated across the room, passing through the wall where the orderly had been waiting.

—

The orderly took the book from her hands. They were not in a sanitarium at all. They were seated across from each other inside a quaint chamber, surrounded by books, as they had been the entire evening. The orderly was the librarian. *He had always been the librarian.* "I suppose you'd call that *Poe*-etic justice," he said, and released volume four into the air.

Prudence Pock watched the book float back to its space on a shelf. There was a blue-green aura pulsating around her body. "I must admit, that's my favorite tale of all." She was especially delighted with the ending.

Caw! Caw! Caw! They were interrupted by the cry of a raven.

Amicus Arcane slid his gloved hand into his vest and checked his pocket watch. "Aah, it's time to choose." And so it was. Time to select the scariest tale of all. And time for another spirit to take over as the mansion's librarian.

The spectral figure of Amicus Arcane appeared on the balcony overlooking the grand hall while down below, ghostly revelers were scaring the night away. Mistresses Granger and Black, the two shrouded apparitions who helped Amicus maintain the library, floated over to Prudence Pock and invited her to join him on the balcony. An announcement was imminent.

The librarian cleared his throat—before returning his throat to his body. "Attention, dear brethren!" The time had come to induct the latest librarian. **Or is it "late librarian"?**

The spirits gathered below—creeping, crawling, slithering—countless souls from different times and different places: three hitchhikers, a mummy, a vampire, a bride with an ax, an old movie star, and a grinning ghost wearing a top hat were among them. Along with a pair of recent arrivals: Shelley and Chris. And, of course, four kids who called themselves the Fearsome Foursome.

A crystal ball containing the bodiless face of one Madame Leota floated up to the balcony. Transfers of power were her department.

The librarian twisted his head to face Prudence. A moment later, the rest of his body followed. "With my deepest sympathies, Prudence Pock, you have been selected. Your untimely demise has provided the scariest tale of all."

There was an uproarious reaction from the grand hall, with special emphasis on *roar*. The spirits, specters, poltergeists, and apparitions—or ghosts, if you prefer—were screeching and shrieking, along with some alarming applause from the ones with hands.

But the warmest reaction came from Willa. Well, relatively warm, for someone minus a pulse. She was thrilled beyond her ghostly capacity. Having the late Prudence Pock as a fellow resident would be like inducting a fifth member to the Fearsome Foursome. Oh, the scary stories they would share for centuries to come!

Prudence floated to the edge of the balcony, hovering above the grisly gathering of ghosts and ghouls. "I am truly honored, Mr. Arcane. I'm flattered beyond words." She paused, looking first at Mistresses Granger and Black, then directly at Willa. "But at this time, I'm afraid I must decline."

The ghosts below grew suspiciously silent. So silent you could hear a heart splat. No one had ever refused such a dishonor. Prudence Pock's announcement was a shock, even to a roomful of shockers. Willa's face dropped; she was so disappointed. Tim politely picked it up for her.

"Is your decision final?" asked Amicus Arcane.

"It is."

"May I ask why?"

A big, bulgy grin returned to Prudence Pock's face. A grin so unsettling even a few ghosts hid their eyes. She had a reason, all right, and she proceeded to explain: "I still have a lot more haunting to do before I retire. There's a patient in a padded room—once a doctor of the mind—who I must continue to visit, night after night, for the rest of his natural life."

Amicus Arcane grinned just a little too wide. "Aah, to haunt the guilty. I can respect that." But the librarian still had a dilemma. "But there is still the matter of my repulsive replacement."

"I have an inspired idea," said Prudence. "There's someone better suited for the job. The perfect keeper of tales is already here among you." And she pointed to Willa.

The librarian nodded. Why hadn't he thought of that? **Because a coroner removed my brain—is that not reason enough?**

"I couldn't," said Willa. "I'm not worthy."

Tim reminded her, "You wanted to be a horror writer when you grew up. This is even better!" He kissed her cheek. "Like you always say, be careful what you wish for."

The phantom organist began playing a funeral dirge as Tim, Noah, and Steve gave Willa a floating escort to the balcony. The librarian smiled as she glided into range. "Mistress Willa, do you accept the position?"

She looked to her friends; they were bouncing, floating,

gloating, giddy with excitement. Noah gave her a shove. "What are you waiting for? Say yes already!"

Willa looked up at the librarian. "Yes already!"

The crowd below went berserk . . . in a good, ghostly way.

Prudence Pock gave Willa a congratulatory hug. "You've got this, kid." She remembered the time. "Oops, I have to fly. My old friend Dr. Ackerman should be getting ready for his bedtime story about now." Prudence gave Willa one last look, along with a reassuring smile, before floating up, up, and away toward Shepperton Sanitarium.

As for the more pressing business of the evening: Madame Leota's head floated between Willa and the librarian. "The spirit of Willa Gaines, do you accept your role as soul keeper of the mansion's tales?"

"I do."

"Will you carry on in your soul capacity to seek out the scariest story of all?"

"I will."

"Then by the powers vested in me, I hereby declare you mansion librarian, for as long as you so shall die."

There was thunderous applause. And thunder, too! Followed by lightning.

The librarian smiled at Willa, this time, for the first time, with a fatherly glint in his eyes.

"Mr. Arcane, I don't know what to say."

"There is nothing to say, Mistress Willa. Let the tales do the talking. Remember: Every spirit has a story. And everyone's story deserves to be heard." He removed the dead carnation from his lapel and placed it in Willa's hair. She looked up to thank him, and in the *clink-tink-clink* of a bracelet . . .

Amicus Arcane was gone.

Willa's friends hooted and hollered, as mischievous boys are wont to do. In her first official capacity as mansion librarian, Willa placed a finger to her lips. "Shhhhhhhh!"

The boys followed her to the library. There were books piled everywhere, new souls to be cataloged. Willa settled into the high-backed chair. "Boys, we have a lot of work ahead of us."

"*We?*"

"Yes, we! Our search continues . . . for the scariest tale of all." The new librarian contemplated the stacks of books surrounding them. Nine hundred ninety-nine tales in all, with room for a thousand. "It's a daunting task," she said; then she thought about it. "Or is it a *haunting* task? I never can get that right."

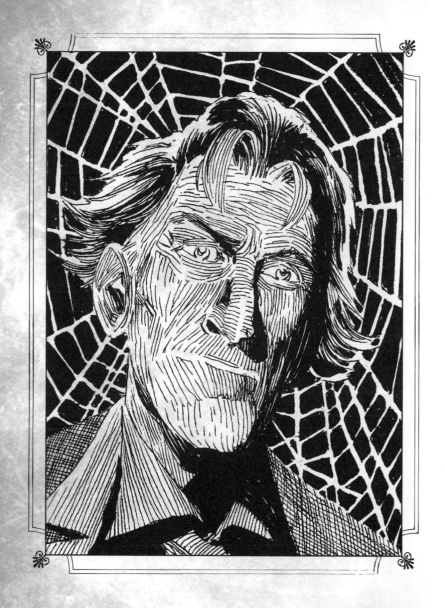

Hereafter
Thoughts

Aah, there you are, foolish mortal.
Congratulations on making it to the bitter end.
You didn't think I was going to leave just yet, did you?
For I have some ghoulishly good news to report.
Unbeknownst to Mistress Willa, or the rest of her Fearsome Foursome,
we have located our most terrifying tale.

It is a horrifying story of supernatural terror.
A tale so terrifying it will cause instant madness.
And that tale, of course, is <u>YOURS</u>.

You've yet to experience the sinister circumstance
that will bring you to our humble abode.
I won't dare spoil the—I mean, your—ending, but rest assured . . .
<u>yours</u> is the scariest story of all!

All the arrangements have been made,
so be sure to bring your death certificate.
Enter freely, and of your own will, and stay for eternity.

Welcome home, foolish mortal.

Welcome to the Haunted Mansion.

Memento mori.

BIOGRAPHIES

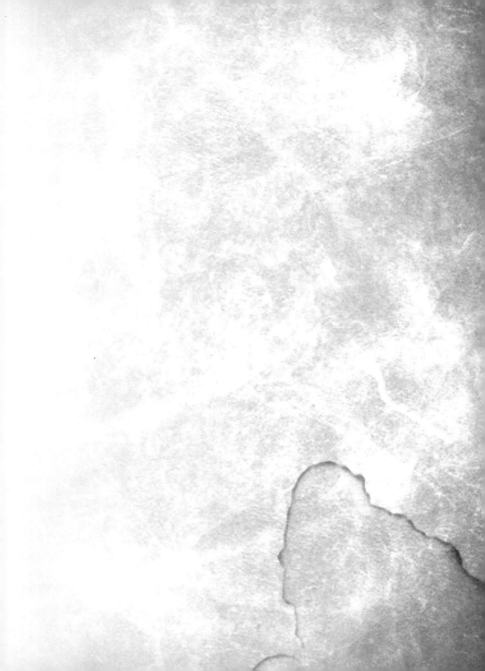

Amicus Arcane *Little is known about the dearly departed Amicus Arcane, save for his love of books. As the mansion librarian, both in this life and in the afterlife, Amicus has delighted in all forms of the written word. However, this librarian's favorite tales are those of terror and suspense. After all, there is nothing better to ease a restless spirit than a frightfully good ghost story.*

John Esposito *When John Esposito met Amicus Arcane on a midnight stroll through New Orleans Square, he was so haunted by the librarian's tales that he decided to transcribe them for posterity. John has worked in both film and television, on projects such as* Stephen King's Graveyard Shift, R. L. Stine's The Haunting Hour, Teen Titans, *and the* Walking Dead *web series, for which he won consecutive Writer's Guild Awards. John lives in New York with his wife and children and still visits with Amicus from time to time.*

Kelley Jones *For the illustrations accompanying his terrifying tales, Amicus Arcane approached Kelley Jones, an artist with a scary amount of talent. Kelley has worked for every major comic book publisher but is best known for his definitive work on Batman for DC Comics. Kelley lives in Northern California with his wife and children and hears from Amicus every October 31, whether he wants to or not.*